SERPENT MOUND

THE NIA RIVERS ADVENTURES BOOK 4

INES JOHNSON

THOSE JOHNSON GIRLS

Some say life moves fast. That's not necessarily true. The speed at which life moves is a matter of perspective.

Parents wrap their offspring in a cocoon of protection that cracks all too soon when the children burst their way out. For the mother and father, it's a blink of the eye. But for the child, independence comes at a snail's pace.

Once they've broken the casing of their parents' hold, the newly-winged adults stutter-step brusquely through life, rushing toward a time when they can slow down. And when that time comes, in the twilight of their years, and their pace is sluggish once more, they look back and lament that they didn't savor what they had as they find themselves hurtling toward an end that they are never quite prepared for.

Such is the human existence. Or so I'd been told over the last couple of millennia by the few thousand human beings I'd asked. It was a rhetorical question: "Where has all the time gone?" For them, the answer was the same, but for someone like me, time had never gone anywhere. It stayed with me.

Life had always moved at a steady pace for me. Every day the world rushed by me in a blur of colors and faces and lights. Most of the time I felt like I was standing still while the world spun. People grew up, grew old, and died in the time it took me to look over my shoulder.

Perhaps that's why I was constantly on a quest to break the speed limits.

My right foot pressed the gas pedal into the floor as I broke one hundred and fifty miles per hour. With the sole of my left foot resting on the floorboard, I felt the gravel kick up at the underbelly of the low-riding car. Looking down at the speedometer, I saw that I crested two hundred miles per hour.

The tires hummed as I urged them to eat more than their share of the asphalt. The engine rumbled, accepting my challenge as I pushed the vehicle to its maximum. The tailpipe roared with delight, not in the least exhausted.

My mouth split in a grin as the adrenaline rushed to my head. I felt my pulse thumping against the leather bindings of the steering wheel. The scenery was a blur of green globules and blue blobs. My short breaths rang in my eardrums as the speed dial ticked up to two hundred and fifty.

"Easy there, tiger," said a deep male voice coming from the passenger seat. "We see your claws. You don't have to bare your teeth as well."

Ignoring my companion, I pressed the gas pedal, aiming to eke out the last twenty miles that the car was reported to go. The Venom GT was the fastest car in the world. And I wanted to go fast right now.

I needed the speed. I needed to bust out of the cocoon that time had wrapped around me from as far back as I could remember. I needed to break free of the casings and hurtle toward whatever was waiting in the twilight for someone like me.

I wanted to outrun life. I wanted to get ahead of the consequences that were on my tail. I wanted to leave this asphalt and take off into the sky.

Instead, I released the gas pedal and pumped the brakes, coming to a screeching halt. Both my body and Tres's slammed forward. My chest smashed into the steering wheel. Tres's chest got intimate with the dashboard.

"Dammit, Nia." He rubbed at the spot on his forehead where he'd contacted the windshield.

I didn't bother to glance at him. I knew he wasn't harmed, just a bit miffed at me and my recklessness. He'd broken no skin. He was nearly unbreakable. Nearly.

Tres turned to me, removing his long forefinger and thick thumb from his brown forehead. The spot where he'd hit his head hadn't even turned dark. No bump would dare form on that proud brow. As he removed his hand from his face, his hair fell over the spot like a silk curtain.

I'd always thought his hair was chestnut, but looking up close I saw that I was wrong. It was more henna, somewhere between a reddish-brown and an orangish-brown. The play of the colors fascinated me, and I stared.

He let me look, making no move to come closer or move away. That was his way with me. He'd give me a moment to decide. But only a moment.

If I hesitated or showed any uncertainty, he'd make my decision for me and make the move that suited him best. Looking in his eyes now, I knew that my moment to choose was almost up. I'd already decided what I would do.

I'd once thought this man was an ogre due to his land-grabbing of historical sites, bulldozing of structures of cultural significance, and building of modern, metallic eyesores. My opinion of his business practices had only shifted slightly. I had no problem admitting that I was entirely wrong about his physicality. An ugly green monster this man was not.

Sure, Tres was big enough to fit the bill. His voice was deep enough to scare grown men. When he smiled, his teeth did this glinting thing that made me feel like he would eat me alive. But any woman would be happy, willing, to be devoured by that wicked grin.

In fact, that grin was getting closer to me. My decision-making time was up, and he was about to take control of the situation and play it to his advantage. His broad shoulders blocked out the sun as he moved into my space. He didn't speak a word with that low, growling voice of his. He didn't need to. I knew his intentions.

I only had one second left. So, I decidedly turned my torso until my back rested against the driver's seat. Facing forward, and away from the advancing passenger, I reached my arms over my head, creating a barrier between the two seats while giving my torso a stretch. My actions also halted Tres's advance.

The car's engine still purred, waiting for my next command. I reached forward and, with a flick of my wrist, turned the key and pulled the fob from the ignition. Swiveling around in the driver's seat, I handed the key back to its owner.

"Thanks," I said to Tres. "I needed that."

His dark gaze raked over my face. I knew he saw the wild glint in my eyes, the flare of my nostrils, and my upper teeth tugging at the corner of my lower lip. I knew that he knew that I was having trouble coming to terms with my feelings for him. We'd gone from enemies to allies and were now knocking on the door of lovers. I'd taken a series of turns on the road with his car, but it was the fast-moving status of our relationship that was giving me whiplash.

"Yeah," said Tres, "I can see you did." His tone was as smooth as the engine of his car. The car had purred at fast speeds, but it had played the same humming tune while it had idled. "Any other thrill ride I can help you with, Dr. Rivers?"

Tres tilted his head against the headrest as he

gazed at me. The gleam in his eyes spoke of patient inevitability. My limbs began to tingle and my legs became restless. I leaned over, turning in the opposite direction, and reached down for the seatbelt. I fumbled a moment before I was able to release the catch.

As I left the car I heard the distinct rumble of laughter coming from the passenger seat. I didn't bother looking behind me to see if he'd follow. Tres liked the chase, and it felt good having someone prowling after me, wanting me.

It felt good being able to laugh with him, to flirt with him, all while a dark cloud floated over our heads. It was nice to forget for a moment that there was any danger on our tail. But it was only a moment.

I took one last look at the Venom GT. It looked like a bug with its headlights resting at slanted angles on the front end. The bumper was assembled in a way that resembled a smirk. The raised back looked like the tail wing of a plane. The bulbous body that could house only two bodies completed the look. I'm sure when it was in motion it resembled a gnat, zipping down the highway so fast that no one could hope to swat it.

Tres caught up beside me. His large hand came

to rest on my lower back as we walked. His fingers didn't flit about like a bug. Neither did they dig into my skin like a tiger's claw. I felt the ridge of his long pinky finger at my sacrum. His thumb glanced off the curve of my waist. His palm followed the movement of my hips.

It was a perfectly normal and benign gesture for a couple. But we weren't a couple. We were...

To be honest, I'm not sure exactly what we were. Because I couldn't entirely remember what we had been. And Tres was very reluctant to tell me about our past.

The men in my life seemed to make that a habit —keeping our past entanglements and indiscretions from me. Zane, the man I had once considered the love of my life, had sworn he kept the past from me in order to protect me. But that secret past had come back to assault us both.

Tres had his own secrets as well as some of mine. But he said he wanted to leave the past behind us and start with a clean slate. Unfortunately for him, my nature was to dig until I knew what the original story said.

"You still haven't told me where we're going," said Tres.

"Yes, I did. I'm taking you home."

"Typically when a woman says she wants to take me home—"

"What?" I snorted. "That's when you run the other way to avoid meeting her parents?"

Tresor Mohandis was an infamous playboy. For the last few decades, he'd been spotted on the arm of, tangling tongues with, and coming out of the boudoirs of some of the world's most beautiful women. As an Immortal, he had to change his name and identity often, but I always recognized his face in a photograph or the tone of his voice in an article.

It wasn't like I was keeping tabs or anything. His affairs were none of my business. If he wanted to gallivant with vapid women every night of the week and twice on Sundays, that was his prerogative. I read the magazines and papers for the news and cultural articles.

"No." Tres grinned, leaning his big body into my shoulder. "If a woman invites me over, I assume we'll be alone and she wants to take me to her bed."

Now, not only was his hand at my back, his body heat was pressed into my side as well. His face hovered above mine as I looked up at him. If he wanted to kiss me, there wasn't much I could do to escape him. There was no seatbelt holding either of us back. There was no barrier between us.

I knew he wouldn't take the advantage. He might move in closer, he might press his point, but at the end of the day, he wanted me to come to him. He'd told me before that this time I'd be the one to make the moves.

I could barely hold my ground as I walked in step with him. My body was raring to go. But something in my mind held me back from dropping the solid green flag to signal him off. If I were honest with myself, which I wasn't ardently trying to be these days, I'd admit that there might be someone holding me back.

I hadn't been with another man in five hundred years. Yep, I said hundreds. Before that, I couldn't remember a single face, though I know there had been a few before Zane. Tres was included in that number. Which meant we'd done it before. I couldn't remember the down and dirty details of doing it with him. But my body remembered that it had liked it.

"We will be alone," I said. "When we get to my place."

He didn't say anything, but I felt a rumble of awareness flare through his body. Standing next to him, I felt overheated. I took a deep breath but still felt frazzled. The tips of my toes and fingers tingled.

I nearly tripped as we climbed a small flight of stairs. Tres held me steady and then pulled me into his body as we mounted the steps.

Finally, we reached our destination and I was able to step away from him. My body cooled and my mind cleared. A good thing too as we approached the aircraft hangar. We climbed the short stair stack that led us into the cockpit of the small seaplane.

"Where's the pilot?" asked Tres.

"You're looking at her." I took the pilot's seat and began my preflight checklist.

Tres stood stock-still on the platform. Even with the headphones I'd just placed over my ears, I heard him gulp.

"What's the matter?" I said. The jitters from just a moment ago were gone now that I was in the driver's seat once more. "Don't you trust me?"

"At two hundred and seventy miles per hour on the ground? It was a little shaky." Tres climbed into the plane and took his seat. "Now you want to go five hundred miles per hour in the air? I've never been comfortable putting my life in someone else's hands."

"You fly all the time. Is it because I'm a woman?"

"No."

"What then?"

"My pilots are on my staff," he said as he strapped himself into the harness. "I pay them a healthy salary to follow my orders. You have never done what I tell you to do."

"That's because I'm not trying to be in your employ."

"What are you trying to be to me, Theta?"

"Buckle up while I figure it out."

CHAPTER TWO

My body jolted in the seat as the turbulence played havoc with the small plane. Beside me, Tres bumped about. His thick fingers gripped the harness belting him into his seat. His jaw clenched and his eyes squinted as though he were traveling through a sandstorm.

I rolled my eyes. As much as the man flew, I knew he'd encountered a little bit of turbulence on a number of occasions. Like choppy waves on an ocean voyage, the choppy air was par for the course of plane travel.

Secretly, I was getting a serious kick out of having this mountain of a man white-knuckling his seat cushion. He was a powerhouse in the corporate world and a no-nonsense businessman when it came to real estate and land development.

We'd battled over the years, with him coming out the victor more times than I'd like to count. Now I had all the power in my grip. My fingers flexed on the controls. I was half-tempted to do a barrel roll. But I wasn't that cruel. Not really.

I reached over and rubbed Tres's knee. He jerked out of my reach.

"Both hands on the wheel, please," he demanded.

"Seriously? I reach out to you and you're telling me to keep my hands to myself?"

"You can take advantage of me when you get us on the ground."

I let out a high-pitched giggle and immediately dipped my chin to swallow the offensive sound. I was not a giggler. I laughed. I smirked. I was even known to guffaw in days gone by. I did not giggle like some society miss.

That wasn't entirely true. Zane knew all the things to say to set me shaking with tinkling laughter. I took a deep breath and got hold of myself. I needed to get my ex out of my mind. Especially since I had decided to make room in there for Tres.

I glanced over at Tres. Of course, at that moment

we hit another rough pocket of air. I took the aircraft up, aiming to find a patch of smooth air to complete our journey. It would probably be best if I spent my mental energy focusing on getting the two of us to our destination intact.

Just last year, I wouldn't have thought that an air crash could've killed me. I had thought that Immortals were impervious to death. I'd been proven wrong, not once, but three times.

I'd learned what we all suspected: that the allergy shared between the twelve of us when we remained in one another's presence for too long could, in fact, kill us. Vau and Epsilon, two older Immortals who had been deeply in love, had met their end that way hundreds of years ago, though I'd only remembered it earlier this year.

Just a week ago, I'd learned that certain magical objects could also end our lives. Yod, an Immortal who liked to interfere in the religious affairs of humans and wreak havoc for his own warped sense of righteousness, had taken a spear to the heart and perished. I had been the one to throw the spear that ended his life. Though he'd asked for it by holding a knife to my bestie's throat, I took no pleasure in his death.

I hadn't known the Spear of Destiny would kill

him. I'd only intended to maim him so that he would release Loren. But when the spear struck his heart, it stopped his life. Now the spear was out in the world with a crazed wizard.

I couldn't focus on Merlin. I had to leave that to his brother, Arthur, and the rest of the Knights of Camelot. I could only handle one apocalyptic danger at a time.

With three of the twelve of us Immortals gone, I'd learned that two more were fated to perish before our past and our purpose here on earth would be revealed to us.

The elderly witch Igraine had seen a vision when I was back at Camelot. The Immortals would be returning to the garden from whence we'd come. I'd seen the garden in a vision, or perhaps it was a memory. There had been lush flowers and deep green pastures. I'd seen all twelve of us together, getting along. Mostly. But Igraine said that only seven of the twelve of us would make it.

Three Immortals were dead, leaving nine walking the earth. There were two Immortals in this plane. I had no intention of being one of the two to go. I had no intention of allowing any more of my kind to meet their end if I could help it. And I had a plan.

My attention was on figuring out what this garden was and where it might be. Perhaps if we could get to it soon, if we could somehow manage to enter it alive and kicking, that would mean that no one else would have to lose their life before we were due back. To figure out the mystery of the garden, I needed to get to the biggest and oldest library of creation myths and biblical works and religious references on the planet. That place was my very own bookshelf on my secret island.

"Is that it?" Tres asked, pointing out the window.

"Yup, that's me."

It was just a short flight from Florida, where we'd taken off, to the Caribbean, where we were about to land. Up ahead the cloud cover broke and my island came into view. There were a number of nondescript islands in the crystal-blue waters of the Caribbean Sea. But my own private island had one distinction. It spelled my name.

"And you used to call me a branding whore," said Tres.

Tresor Mohandis had his name on everything. His private plane. His massive yacht. All of his buildings and holdings. Other than signing my name to documents and artifacts throughout history, this was the only other item in the world that bore my name.

Each of the twelve Immortals had been branded with a symbol on their back. My symbol looked like the Hebrew or Aramaic number nine. My island was shaped like a U. A sandy beach formed the bottom half of the symbol. A small mountain range extended from the top, slicing diagonally into a forest. I'd named the little slice of paradise Noohra, which was a Galilean word that meant "light."

I pulled back on the throttle and the plane leveled on the horizon. As I pulled on the yoke, we descended and came to a smooth landing in the water.

I'd found this place in the early 1500s. I'd been sailing from the New World and headed back to Spain when pirates attacked the ship I was on. The marauders took one look at my brown skin and decided to enslave me. Unfortunately for them, I was superhuman. I managed to get away by going overboard and drifted at sea for a few days. I wound up here on my little island of light.

This was my Fortress of Solitude. The place where I kept all of my treasures and secrets. I'd never brought anyone here. Though somehow, Zane knew about this place. Maybe I'd brought him in the past? I couldn't remember.

Before our five-hundred-year dating stint, we'd been together seven other times. My memories of those times had been nonexistent two months ago. But now, little by little, things were coming back to me.

I gave myself another shake. Now was not the time to be thinking about Zane and what we once shared. I was here with Tres. I had chosen Tres.

I turned to Tres as we debarked from the plane. He took the place in. As his dark gaze swept across my private beach, I realized I was anxious to know what he thought of my home.

He said nothing as we waded through the water to get to dry land. Intelligent eyes took in the surroundings. The beach was pristine with white sands. The forest kept its distance and hid the interior with a curtain of green.

"This place is completely untouched," he said.

"Yeah."

"How far are we from the mainland?"

"A couple hundred miles or so?" I looked at him again, noting that intelligence had turned to calculation. I shoved his chest. "If you even think of bringing one of your bulldozers anywhere near—"

"Hey, hey." Tres caught my hand in his grip and smiled. "Occupational hazard. You look at a pile of dirt and want to dig it up. I look at a pile of dirt and want to build a fort. It's our nature."

His tone was soothing, but he'd already awakened the beast in me. He swooped in with his other hand and wrapped it around my waist, bringing me flush with his body. The heat of him made me melt. Just a bit.

We had been at odds for hundreds of years, and it kept coming back to this. How in the world were we supposed to make a relationship work when our very ideals stood apart?

"I know that your bringing me here is a big deal, and I honor that," Tres said. "I would never violate that trust."

He brought his body closer to mine. That same heat flared. The water that had seeped into my clothing evaporated.

"It was a slip of the tongue," he said, his voice in a low register. "My tongue does that from time to time. It's not always a bad thing."

His head was over mine. His lips angled in a way that all I needed to do was tilt my head and taste. I inhaled deeply, and the sweet, woody smell of frankincense lapped against the tip of my tongue.

The smell rolled off of Tres like waves in the ocean. The moisture in my mouth increased and I swallowed, taking down more of the spicy scent that made me warm from the inside out.

The incense was traditionally used in religious and burial ceremonies. It was most noted for being one of the gifts of the Three Wise Men at the birth of Christ. But it was also used as a burnt offering to a god.

I had nearly made up my mind to tilt my chin up and take in his offering when he stepped back.

"Now," he said. "Where's this house of yours?"

My voice was too shaky to use so I raised my arm and pointed.

Tres's gaze followed my trajectory. "Through the dense swamp and into the forest? Of course."

I'd forgotten. Tresor Mohandis wasn't one for the outdoors. Mr. Broody Billionaire liked the creature comforts of the modern era. There were tons of creatures here, and he'd have to contend with them all before we got to the comfort of my home.

"I don't suppose you stashed a car on this island?" he asked. "Or a golf cart? Maybe a mule?"

"Nope, we're hoofing it." I found my footing and headed through the sand.

Behind me, I heard Tres sigh, but he caught up.

"I don't understand your distaste for roughing it," I said as we trudged into the foliage. "We've been alive since before indoor plumbing."

"Why do you think I'm so obsessed with building and renovations? I believe in luxury."

"Not interested in being one with nature?"

"Why?" His nose crinkled in disgust. It was kind of adorable.

"To reconnect."

"Without Wi-Fi?" His dark brows dipped in distaste.

"I love being outside," I said. "Sleeping under the stars. Hearing the sounds of nature."

"I've also known you to like a good spa."

"True," I acknowledged. "I guess I like both. The best of both worlds."

I came to a dead halt. I inhaled, my eyes widening as I took in my surroundings. My attention was diverted by a flash of movement in the green.

"What?" Tres asked, stopping beside me, his large body alert. "What is it?"

"Dinner."

"Really?" groaned Tres. "We're eating rodents?"

I took off after the white blur. The opossum couldn't outrun me, but it was smaller and could get through the brush quicker than I could.

I leaped up into the air, over thicket and brush, and landed on the opposite side of the marsupial. It zigged around and headed back the other way.

I saw it surface on the other side. I jumped up vertically, catching a tree branch. Swinging like Tarzan, I landed right in front of our meal and pulled my blade from my hip. Before I could extend my weapon, a dagger struck the animal dead between its eyes. I looked up and watched Tres swagger toward his kill.

"I said I liked luxury, but I haven't forgotten my roots." He picked up the slain animal with a frown, then faced me, resignation on his face. "You're the only woman I'd go native for."

CHAPTER THREE

I reached the hidden structure at the edge of the mountain that was the only place I could ever remember calling home. The log cabin blended into the scenery so that, in the unlikely event of a passerby, it would look like it was a part of the landscape, just as I had designed.

If someone came upon this island by chance, they would look at the dense forest and marshy land and likely think twice about venturing inland. If they did manage to brave the elements, they would have to look real hard to see my home. But like I said, it was highly unlikely that anyone would even get this far inland if they stumbled across the island.

"You built that?"

I turned to look over my shoulder at Tres. He had

the dead opossum slung over his shoulder along with his designer satchel that he'd brought along for the ride. I hadn't brought anything with me. I never did. I was quite happy to go native while at home. And by native, I meant naked and living off the land.

I'd told Tres that we'd be gone for a day or two. So, he'd packed. Of course, he'd brought work with him. He cocked his head as he looked at my home, likely realizing that there was no electricity to be found. And worse, no Wi-Fi connection.

He tilted his head from side to side. Watching his scrutiny, I felt instantly territorial. Having Tres look at my Fortress of Solitude was like having him look at me naked.

Yes, I know he'd seen me naked. I just couldn't remember it. Entirely.

Every once in a while I caught flashes of our time together. I was dressed in a peplos, a flowing gown worn in the time of ancient Greece. Or nothing at all.

In those memories, Tres had his arms around me, embracing me with care and tenderness. Or he had his arms out in front of me, flailing in irritation and frustration. The looks on our faces was always intense, either filled with passion and desire or fire and anger.

Had there ever been any middle ground between

us? Any time when we'd relaxed in each other's presence with no agendas, no battles?

I heard the echo of the answer *yes* from somewhere deep inside. But I couldn't bring forth a shred of proof in my mind. Why would I lock those memories away?

Likely for the same reason I had locked away any memory of Zane from before the 15th century. Victims of trauma often cordoned off parts of their brains to protect the psyche. I'd pushed away the memories of China where Epsilon and Vau had died. I'd pushed away memories of Demeter and her siblings after I learned how they'd come into this world. What was so terrible that I'd decided it was best to forget about Tres other than these few polarizing moments?

His gaze met mine in the middle of the forest. The clarity in his dark eyes told me that he knew the answers. He remembered the good times as well as the bad ones.

I parted my lips to ask. His throat worked as he swallowed past his Adam's apple. His gaze moved from the question in my eyes to the silence of my tongue, and then back again. The only sound that slipped past my bottom lip was a shaky sigh.

I cleared the punctuation mark from my eyes,

leaving behind a trail of unanswered questions. They'd hold. I closed my mouth and reached for his hand.

"Come on," I said as I guided him down the path that led to my most sacred place.

We came to the threshold of my door. As was my habit, I relinquished all weapons and placed them on the doorstep. This was my sanctuary. No weapons inside. No shoes either.

Watching Tres pull off his boots was incredibly intimate. In my memories, I had at least tucked away a detailed mapping of every part of his body. But watching him place his boots next to mine and then stand barefoot and ready to enter my abode made my heart soften.

My fingers shook as I reached out to touch the metal door latch. The breeze coming off the waters was light, but it made me shiver. My stomach rumbled, and my head filled with fog.

I couldn't understand why such a simple thing as letting a man into my home was having such an effect on me. But Tres was no ordinary man. And this wasn't the first time we'd done this.

I'd let him in before. I'd let him past my defenses and brought him close to me. I searched my instincts for a sign of whether I was making a mistake repeating this process.

Tres's hand landed on mine. His chest pressed against my shoulders. "Let me in?"

Oh, the subtext of it all. I knew he wanted to be let inside more than my house. He wanted to be let inside my mind, inside my body, and probably inside my heart. It was a tall order. But now, with all those intimate places put in perspective, I could handle the housewarming.

I opened the door. It was dark inside as the trees blocked out most of the sunlight. I flipped a switch just inside the door, and the solar generator cranked on.

We waited just a step across the threshold as my home slowly became illuminated. My bare feet warmed the cold floor. I looked down to see that Tres's heavy stance made the floorboards creak.

With our eyes adjusted, I led my guest further into the room. There were only two rooms. Well, only two rooms that were visible. We were standing in the larger of the two. This was not only my sanctuary, it's where I came to work.

I'd spent my life uncovering the past, piecing together stories, digging up artifacts to fill the gaps of not only my memory but also that of human history. It was my obsession. It was my passion. It was the only thing I had to offer the world.

It was all laid out in this large room. On the table were the last artifacts I'd been working on. There were three protective glass cases on my desk. Beneath each case was one of the Qumran Scrolls. They were why I'd come home.

The Qumran Scrolls, better known as the Dead Sea Scrolls, were widely known across the world as the oldest records of biblical manuscripts. The documents were over two thousand years old. Many of the parchments were on display in museums around the world. But these three scrolls I had purposefully sequestered when the artifacts were found back in the 1940s. Why? Because these three pieces spoke of twelve immortal beings.

I'd been trying to figure out who wrote the scrolls, since it hadn't been me. They were written partly in Hebrew, partly in Aramaic, with a few symbols I didn't quite understand thrown in the mix. Discovering the author of the scrolls no longer took precedence for me.

Now I needed to see if the scrolls spoke of a garden or paradise. I needed to find out if they held any clues that would lead me to the place Igraine saw in her vision. I needed to know if they could help me save two more of my kind from meeting their end.

"Are you going to show me around?"

I jumped at the sound of Tres's voice. I'd forgotten he was with me. I was so used to being here alone, to doing much of my work alone. Except for this last six months, when I'd been with Loren. And it was impossible to forget that she was around. She never shut up. But Tres didn't appear to mind my silences. Likely because he could brood with the best of them.

"This is pretty much it," I said, and then promptly bit my tongue at the lie.

There were two more parts to my home. I walked him to the room I felt most comfortable showing him: the entrance of my bedroom. I'd made the four-poster bed out of tree trunks from the forest and stuffed the mattress with dried leaves and animal hides. Looking at the bed, it hit me: I would be sleeping with Tresor Mohandis tonight. Maybe showing him this room wasn't the safest bet.

It shouldn't be a big deal. I'd slept with him before. But I only seemed able to remember one time.

I remembered the darkness of the sky pinpointed by starlight. I remembered him walking toward me, bare-chested. I remembered the look on his face. His brows had been arched high into his hairline, as though he couldn't believe it was happening.

I never seemed to see that scene in order. I saw him doing mundane things like biting at his lip or tugging at his earlobe or flexing his thick muscles or striding toward me with those powerful thighs.

"Nia?"

"Hmm?" I blinked.

Tres grinned, likely certain he knew the trajectory of my thoughts. "Is it okay if I set my bag in here?"

I looked at his expensive piece of luggage. It looked out of place in my frontier-woman home as he held it over my bed.

"Sure." I nodded.

He dropped the bag with a soft thud. The sound reverberated in my eardrum. I stared at the bag, wondering at its implications.

"No indoor plumbing, I see?"

I turned to him, frowning. "You can go in nature."

Tres held up his hands in a *stop* motion. "I'm not judging, just observing."

"Sorry, this isn't the Four Seasons."

"I don't need the Four Seasons."

"I'm proud of this place," I said. "I built it with my own two hands."

"You did a wonderful job." He took a step toward me, his hands outstretched. His powerful thighs strode forward, his feet were quiet now on the floorboards.

"But?" I stepped back, nearing the exit. My arms crossed over my chest. My heel thumped as it drove into the ground.

"No 'but,'" Tres said. He looked over my shoulder out into the main room. His gaze went contemplative. "I mean, I could help you spruce up the place."

"There will be no sprucing." I yanked my arms from my chest and balled my hands into fists. "I like everything just the way it is."

Tres turned his head and found my gaze. He was silent for a moment, searching my face. My anger deflated like an untied balloon, but I kept my fists balled, trying to hold on to my airs.

"Why are you picking a fight, Theta?"

"Why are you picking at my home?"

"Is it because I put my things in your bedroom?"

I couldn't help glancing at the bag sitting at the

foot of my bed. A bed only I had slept in. So far as I could remember.

"I didn't say I was sleeping with you," he added.

"What?" My gaze tracked back to Tres. "Are you sleeping outside? Or on the floor in my office?"

"No, I'm sleeping with you."

I cocked my head in confusion.

"Let me be clear," he said, taking the few steps to close the distance between us. "I'm sleeping in your bed. But I haven't decided if I'm ready to have sex with you yet."

My head tilted to the other side, still shrouded in confusion. "Excuse me?"

Tres grinned, but it wasn't the smug grin I'd come to know and loathe. His gaze raked over my face like he was looking for something. By the time he focused on my eyes, I wasn't sure if he'd found it or not.

"I want more than something physical with you," he said.

"What do you want?"

He placed his large palm on my chest.

I looked down. My breast? He wanted my breast? Honestly, I'd taken him for an ass man.

"More," he said, pressing his hand into my beating heart. "I want more."

The bag at the foot of my bed was forgotten with that single word. I had decided to explore a relationship with Tres. And, yes, that included the physical. What I had not considered was putting my heart in play. It was still on a massive time-out as it struggled to let go of a five-hundred-year love affair.

Sex, I could do. But love? I let out another shaky breath as Tres walked around me.

"No stove either?" I heard him call out. "That doesn't surprise me. Why don't you go get to work while I play domestic."

He walked out the front door. I glanced behind me at the other door. The one I hadn't shown him. The one where all my secrets lay. I turned from that hidden door and went to my desk to do as he said. I got down to work.

CHAPTER FOUR

The last artifact I'd been working on lay under protective glass. It was a few pages of the Dead Sea Scrolls.

They'd been found in the mid-twentieth century but were likely written before the second century. Locals in Qumran had found the artifacts wrapped in linen and stored in jars in eleven different caves. Many believed the scrolls had been placed in the caves to hide them from the advancing Roman army during a Jewish revolt in 68 AD.

The authors were likely Jewish scholars. The scrolls were an eight-hundred-plus-page manuscript written on papyrus. Most of the writings were from the books of what most humans knew to be the Hebrew Bible, what

Christians called the Old Testament. The rest of the writings were religious texts and secular writings like laws, catalogs, war chronicles, and battle playbooks.

There was a small portion of the scrolls that humans hadn't been able to identify. I had three pages of those documents.

The first two pages spoke of the Elohim, or what was more commonly referred to by humans as angels. Most civilizations with godly figures spoke of helpers to their spiritual rulers. These helpers, or angels, were called many names.

The Hindu called them devas, entities that controlled the elements but were not worshipped. In Islam, they were known as Malaikah, and they acted as intermediaries between humans and the divine. The Grauashi were also protectors and guides in Zoroastrianism.

The first of the Qumran Scrolls before me spoke of ten types or classes of Elohim. There were the Ophanim, who were described as the many-eyed ones and the wheels, if that made any sense. It didn't to me.

The scroll went on to describe more classes, like the Hashmallim, or the amber ones. The way the author used the word "amber" made me suspect he was talking about electricity, which was around long before Benjamin Franklin.

The Malakim were messengers. The Erelim were the justice-bearers. There was also mention of the Ishim, who were in charge of mortal affairs.

Included amongst the ranks were also the Seraphim and Cherubim. But unlike the human rosy-faced depictions of fat babies on one shoulder and horned devils on the other, there was no stratification of good or evil. These beings were classified by the jobs they did, not their personality traits.

The scroll told of the snake-like Seraphim, who all had six wings on their person. The Cherubim were the protectors of Eden. That line caught my eye.

Eden. The garden. But there was no mention in the three scrolls of where the fabled garden might lay.

Outside my home, I heard the crackling of a fire. I stood and peered out the window. Tres had skinned our dinner and was now stripping off the choicest bits of meat. I watched a moment and admired his handiwork. Mr. Broody Billionaire was pretty handy with a knife. But I knew that already from our time fighting in China, and then again in Mosul.

He'd taken off his shirt. I wasn't sure if it was to protect the fabric or to give me an eyeful. For a man of leisure, Tres's body was cut from finely-chiseled and expertly-sculpted marble.

My upper lip felt moist. I jerked from the glass to see that I'd had my nose pressed against it. The condensation fogged a hole at the center of the window.

Tres chose that moment to look up. I jerked back even further. But the smirk at the corner of his mouth told me he'd seen me.

Instead of giving him anything more to gloat about, I turned back to my desk. Bending my head over the third scroll, I set about making sense of the symbols and shapes of the Aramaic and Hebrew languages. Lines and squiggles reformed in my head until I saw letters, then words, then sentences, and finally meanings. The third document was a creation story.

Every human culture had a creation story, an explanation for how the world came to be and the storyteller's place in it. These tales were as old as time. They didn't all start with the biblical story of the seven days of creation. Still, it was surprising how similar the stories were across cultures and across the globe.

In the *Enuma Elish*, written by the Babylonians in the Akkadian language, the gods Apsu and Tiamat were the patriarch and matriarch of a highly dysfunctional family—like most gods. The title, *Enuma Elish*, translated to "when on high." Apsu, the patriarch of the story, was made of fresh water, whereas Tiamat, his feminine counterpart, was formed of the salty, bitter water. Ladies, take note of a trend forming.

Anyway, the two primordial gods were united in the beginning in what was known as chaos. In the chaos, Apsu and Tiamat gave birth to the gods. But these young gods were loud and unruly once they were brought out of the chaos. Their loud and raucous ways got on the sweet-watered nerves of Apsu. And so, in a flash of Greek drama, he plotted to kill the kids.

When Tiamat found out, she told the godlings. The rebel youth turned on Apsu and killed him, which made Tiamat salty. She went to war against her kids for killing her baby daddy. One of these patricidal gods, Marduk, shot her with a bow and arrow, rending her in two, thus creating the heavens and earth. From the tears in Tiamat's eyes, the rivers of the Tigris and Euphrates flowed. The godlings then made humans out of the carcasses of their parents.

Believe it or not, that story is par for the course. There are a lot of creation myths that say the world was created out of the severed or mutilated body of a mother goddess. There was a lot of violence done to women's bodies for birth, food, housing, and general sacrifice.

Selu, the first woman in the Cherokee creation story, was killed by her sons so that her body would produce corn for them to eat. The Greeks' beginning was of Eros, the primordial egg, hatching and sending half his shell up to become the sky, which became Uranus. The other half became the earth, or Gaia. I think we all know what happened when those two met in the middle and started having little Titan babies that came to dwell on Mount Olympus.

My favorite creation stories, likely due to my love of language, were the ones that said the universe began with a sound. The Hindus believed the universe began with the sound of Om. West Africans believed the world began with the word Yo.

Dismembered deities and filicidal offspring aside, there were other things creation stories had in common: a flood and a garden.

Most of these were similar to the Noahic myth of

a deluge wiping out most of humanity and the animal kingdom. But note how they are all local to each culture telling the tale. For example, in the Hindu flood myth, Shraddhadevu Manu saved his family and seven mages from a flood by building a boat that carried them to safety in India.

Zeus reportedly caused the flood of ancient Greece in a fit over a sacrifice he didn't like. By the way, I could totally see that happening, having met the god in real life. But still, having met the god of thunder in the flesh, I knew this wasn't true. There was a reason to believe that the flood in ancient India, as well as the flood in ancient Greece, were both natural phenomena that only affected their little corner of the globe.

I wasn't so sure what to make of the Norse creation story where the frost giant, Bergelmir, along with his family, were the only survivors of a deluge of blood. After the god, Odin, and his brothers killed Bergelmir's father, Bergelmir was set adrift on a river of blood. There were no red rivers that I knew of in Scandinavia.

Then there was the Chinese myth, which had always irked me. Not only because there was actual archaeological evidence to support the story's claims, but also because of who it involved: the Xia

Dynasty. There was much evidence of the Yellow River bursting its banks. Some of those stories were even documented—by me. But, again, those floods were contained. Not worldwide.

In fact, most flood myths were locally contained and pointed to different time periods. They could all be explained as natural phenomena and disasters.

That left the garden stories. In the majority of the garden stories, there was an initial paradise, an idyllic world where humans inevitably messed up and fell off the cliff. God's most favored creation always lost their innocence in some way and were shoved down into misery.

Unlike the flood stories that marked a clean slate from mistakes, in the garden stories humans were searching for a foundation for existence, a reason for being. Like a newborn who needed swaddling, they needed the confinement of boundaries they could not break in order to understand their purpose in the big scary world. No matter how old the culture, these stories persisted.

They were found in the biblical Book of Genesis, in the Holy Quran, in Native American folklore, in the Mesopotamian *Epic of Gilgamesh*.

In the Bible, Adam and Eve were forbidden to eat from the tree of knowledge. When, inevitably, they did, they knew death. They were then summarily kicked out of the garden.

In the Mesopotamian myths, there was a garden and a tree. But there were no forbidden fruits. There was, however, talk of a plant stolen by a serpent that could restore youth.

In the Babylonian myths, Adam or Adapa was invited to eat of the fruit. But he didn't because he thought it was a trick. Unfortunately, the joke was on him, because the food would've granted him immortality.

In the final Qumran Scrolls before me, it didn't speak of humans. It spoke of demigods, Elohim. It told that these beings came up from the garden and saw that the daughters of man were beautiful. The text said that these beings lay with the human women and then returned to the garden.

I noted that it didn't say which of the ten types of beings. It used the collective term. It also used the specific word *Eden* as the name of the garden.

Eden meant "delight" in Hebrew. Edinu meant "plain" in Akkadian. Edin meant "steppe" in Sumerian. What if this garden were an actual place? What if that tree or that fruit or the waters were some sort of fountain of youth? What if these beings, these Elohim, were living creatures sequestered away in this garden.

Could I be the child of an angel?

Aleph, the oldest of my kind, had always believed that to be a fact. I never gave it much credence, because I didn't believe in God with the big G.

I'd met many gods with the little G over my lifetime. Gods like the Olympians, and the witches and knights of Camelot, and animal shifters of the Americas—we were all beings with enhanced abilities and powers. I hadn't known about all of these beings my whole life. I'd only met the Balam of Central America about a thousand years ago when I began venturing into the southern parts of the New World.

What if there were more supernatural beings living in secret? What if there was a way to get to this garden? There had to be if they came from there.

I remembered the scriptures had said that the angels came from on high down to earth. But as I looked at the scroll laid out before me, I saw mention of coming down. Looking again, I saw that it said the Elohim came up from the garden.

Up?

My mind swirled with every story I ever heard,

read, and wrote. One story bubbled up to the surface. There was a story written about a thousand years ago. It told a tale of two twin gods who came up from a garden to make mischief on earth.

I hadn't thought about the story in years. Mainly because I hadn't believed the two tricksters who'd told me the story. But thinking back on it now, it fit.

I looked over to the hidden doorway that led down to my vault. The scroll I'd written nearly a thousand years ago was down there in my collection. I stood and took a step toward the door.

"Nia?" Tres called.

I turned, placing my back in front of the concealed doorway.

Tres poked his head in the doorway. "Possum's ready," he said with a smile.

I headed toward the threshold and joined him outside. Bringing him to my home was one thing. I wasn't ready to share all my secrets. The scroll would have to wait.

CHAPTER FIVE

The meat was surprisingly good. Tres had ventured into the forest and found a few side items to go with our main dish of marsupial. On the plates were boiled kale and fresh blackberries.

He'd not only gone into the forest, I saw he'd gone back down to the beach as well. The meat was garnished with seaweed, which worked great as a salt substitute.

He'd even set the table. We sat outside on two tree stumps that he'd brought closer together around a larger stump. There were even reeds placed over the bark as a tablecloth. I had to admit that I was a bit shocked at the display.

I didn't miss the smug smile on his face. He'd done a good job. The last time we were out in the wilderness he'd had trouble getting on his horse. His designer clothes had gotten destroyed on the first day. But he was holding his own out here.

"Tresor Mohandis, domestic god."

"Sounds about right." He grinned as he handed me into my stumpy seat. "I dine in nothing less than four-star restaurants."

I picked up my main course and took a bite. The meat was perfectly cooked with the tender bits needing only a few seconds of chewing before the morsels slid down my throat. The veggies and fruit were the perfect complements. Fresh spring water completed the course. A five-star chef couldn't have done it better.

"How long have you had this place?"

"A few hundred years."

"I've never stayed any place that long."

"What?" I said. "You don't have a Fortress of Solitude?"

He frowned.

"You know, like Superman?"

"I don't keep up with pop culture. It changes too much to hold my attention. But no. No fortress. I like to be mobile."

"Like a true desert nomad?"

Tres tipped his glass with a matching quirk of his

lip and eyebrow. I froze in the act of bringing my own cup to my mouth. I'd seen him do that very same action before.

A memory flashed in my mind with Tres and myself in the sand. We were not on the Mediterranean of Greece. There were no white Doric columns reaching into the sky. Instead, the buildings on the horizon were shades of brown, desert sands. Reaching up to the skies were terraced ziggurats.

I stood next to Tres, wrapped in a woolen shawl, a clay cup in my hands that I raised to my lips in mimic of his motions. Tres grinned, quirking his brow and lip before downing his drink.

He was not dressed in the traditional chiton. He wore a wrap skirt around his strong thighs, indicating he was a man of the noble class of ancient Mesopotamia.

In my vision, I focused on the building before us. But from the outside looking in on my vision, I focused on the man. Tres wore the same prideful grin on his face as he pointed up to the sunbaked bricks being laid by dozens of men in loincloths. I had to assume he was the architect of the building.

As the vision-me admired his work, Tres admired my profile. We stood apart at a respectable distance. He made no move to close that gap. In fact, he looked around as though expecting someone to happen upon us. His eyes narrowed shrewdly as he scanned the crowd. Not finding what he searched for, his gaze flicked down in what looked like guilt. But by the time his eyes found me again, that shame was gone.

Vision-me turned from the building to him with a friendly smile on my face. Tres had wiped the desire off his own countenance and replaced it with a similar cordial look.

"What's going on in that head of yours?" he asked.

I blinked, pulling myself out of the vision and coming back to the present. The truth spilled from my mouth. Well, a partial truth did. "I've been having dreams."

"You've been having naughty dreams about me, Dr. Rivers?"

"I can't always tell if they're memories or not."

One side of his face tensed, and he clenched his fist. Then he exhaled slowly and leaned forward. He opened his hands like an offering. I'd seen him do that before, too.

I felt my mind doing a wavy flashback motion.

Tres and I stood together again. But we still weren't in Greece.

I could tell the time was a different era. I was dressed in a colorful linen tunic pinned at my shoulder in the style of an ancient Grecian woman. My feet were sandaled, and over my forearms was a different shawl made of Persian silk.

Tres stood behind me as we both looked out a window at a building in the shape of a horse.

"Why don't you tell me what they were," Tres said, pulling me back again from my reverie. "These visions, or memories."

I hesitated. For Immortals, memories were a form of currency. Animals concerned themselves with food, water, and shelter. Humans fought over land and money. For beings who had lived as long as we did, beings who had more experiences than a brain could contain, memories of the past could be used as leverage.

"I remember a horse," I said. "A large wooden horse, like a building."

Tres grimaced.

"And you had that same look on your face. I remember your riding skills from China, so I'm assuming you didn't build the structure?"

"No, I'm not fond of horses."

I waited. "That's not exactly an answer."

"You didn't ask a question."

"Here's a question," I said. "How many times do you remember us being together?"

"Together-together?"

"I don't need a blow-by-blow."

His grin was sharp, shark-like. I felt my face heat. Was I freaking blushing?

"I just mean how many times have we...dated?" I asked.

"Dated..." He said the word as though he was testing its meaning.

"Been a couple?" I clarified.

Tres wobbled his head left and right as though he were balancing the weight of the memories in his head. "Twice."

"Counting now, you mean?"

"No."

I waited. It was like pulling teeth getting answers. "So, Greece and..."

"Technically, we weren't *together* in Greece."

"But we were in Greece. I remember temples. I remember looking out over the Mediterranean Sea while you held me in your arms and I—"

I stopped talking abruptly. I'd revealed far too much and felt exposed. Looking up at Tres, I saw that a small smile played at his face as though he had the same memories.

"We met again in Greece," he said.

"Again?"

He nodded. "While I was doing some work for King Menelaus. We rekindled our friendship and became...closer."

"We'd been friends before?"

His nod was careful, measured. His chin didn't dip low enough to reach his chest, as though he was a bit uncertain about the veracity of that statement. "You decided to return with me to the city I was staying in back in Turkey."

"What city?"

"Troy."

Pieces started to shift around in my head as memories became unlocked. I remembered sailing over the seas. I remembered armies. I remembered more clearly that large wooden horse.

It had not been a building. I remembered watching it being rolled into the city of Troy, a gift from the Greek army after they conceded in battle.

"No." I shook my head. "That's just a myth." I'd never bought into that story of the Trojan horse. Mainly because I knew too many Greeks. They never conceded.

Tres said nothing.

"That story's never been proven. In fact, no one has ever proven that the author, Homer, existed."

Tres raised an eyebrow.

"There's no evidence of the city of Troy. It's a—"

"Myth?"

But the more I denied it, the more the memories flooded back to my mind. And I saw... Zane.

I remembered the Spartan king Menelaus. I remembered dining with him, sitting beside Demeter. I remembered trying to get drunk, which was a tough task for an Immortal with a superhuman metabolism. I remembered dancing and flirting and drinking and crying on Demeter's shoulder. I was acting like a girl who'd just had a bad break-up.

In the corner of my mind, standing in the back of the room, I saw Zane. He watched me, his face solemn and resigned.

I remembered representatives of a Persian emissary entering the room. Among them were Bet and Tres. Bet set about ignoring Demeter while both of them kept tabs on the other out of the corner of their eyes. Tres made a beeline for Zane. Zane's eyes lit as Tres embraced him. Then Tres turned and found me. That same flicker of guilty desire shone in his gaze for just a brief second before he schooled his features and gave me a friendly wave.

I shut my eyes, trying to turn off my mind and the flood of memories. When I opened them again, Tres watched me silently. His body still leaned forward. His hands flexed open and closed as he waited for me to speak.

"No one's ever called me Helen." It was the only thing I could come up with. I could remember all my various names and aliases. "That war couldn't have been about me."

"It wasn't," he said simply. "Greece and Turkey have been at each other's throats for a long time, you know that."

I did. The Greek Goddess Demeter and the Immortal Bet had a love-hate relationship that had scarred the region for millennia.

"When you left with me it provided a convenient excuse for a fight," said Tres.

"But you and Zane? You were friends?" In my vision, the happiness of their greeting had been palpable. It felt like they were more than friends. Like they were family.

"We were friends." Tres nodded. His eyes took on that same sheen of shame with a hint of sorrow. And then he rolled his shoulders back. "You've always been Zayin's Achilles' heel."

Achilles?

"The horse wasn't his idea," said Tres. "But yeah, that's why I hate horses."

Tres clenched his fist and leaned back. I rocked forward, lowering my head until it was in line with my heart. That didn't stop the nausea or the light-headedness. I took a deep breath and lifted my head in search of more answers.

"You said Greece was the second time we were together," I said. "When was the first time?"

Tres hesitated. And then he spit it out. "Mesopotamia."

"What happened there? Are you going to tell me that I was the cause of the war between Sumer and Elam?"

The war between Sumer and Elam was the first recorded war in history. It took place around 2700 BCE.

"I don't remember much that far back," he said. "But I think that's enough history for today. I'd like to live in the present for the rest of the night."

He reached his hand out to me. I looked down at it. It was a short distance.

"I feel like the past will always be between us," I said.

"Past events? Or a person from your past?"

I opened my mouth and then closed it. I leaned forward, opening my palm, and then I rocked back and put my hands in my lap.

I looked up at Tres. I expected him to be angry, but he wasn't. He was thoughtful.

"I know that you love him," Tres said. "I sure as hell know how he feels about you."

He scratched at his chin. He'd been in the wild for less than twenty-four hours and already a five o'clock shadow was making its way around his chin.

"Zane and I have a complicated past, too," Tres said. "I'm not trying to compete with what's between the two of you. Not anymore. I made that mistake before."

Tres leaned forward on the makeshift table and made a come-hither motion with his fingers. I offered him my hand. He rubbed my fingernails and then my knuckles. Then he folded my fingers into the palm of his hand.

"You keep going back to him, but you also keep breaking up with him and forgetting he existed. That's the definition of insanity, you know— repeating the same actions and expecting a different outcome. Maybe you and I can try something different?"

"Like what?"

He brought my fingertips to his lips and kissed each one. He released my hand and leaned back. "Let's try telling the truth."

"You first."

Tres grinned. "The truth is I tried to steal you away from my best friend. Twice. The truth is I've wanted you since the first time I saw you, which happened to be when you were wrapped in Zane's arms. The truth is you're the only woman who has ever gotten under my skin. And the truth is I may have taken my anger of losing you out by dismantling and bulldozing a few ancient sites that I knew meant something to you."

I gasped and pulled my hands back. He'd been doing well until he got to that last truth.

"Come back here, Theta."

I balked. But he reached across the table and caught my wrists.

"I'm sorry," he said. "I'd like to try again. No secrets. No hiding. No lies."

I couldn't look away. His voice and his gaze and his hold were so full of contrition.

"It's over between me and Zane," I said. "He made it perfectly clear."

Tres's eyes widened as he looked down at me. "He broke up with you this time? That's never happened before."

But it had happened. And I was moving on. Right now.

I swallowed. Then I rose from my seat. As I took the first step, Tres met me halfway.

He ran his fingers down the side of my face. Memories swirled in his dark eyes. When his lips touched mine, it felt as though a key turned and memories flooded to the forefront of my mind.

My body knew this man. Our movements were like driving a familiar route on autopilot. Like dancing to the steps of a familiar tune.

But all too soon, he pulled away from me.

"Are we still going slowly?" I asked.

"Not slowly. Just differently." He captured my lips again. "I realize you might not be ready to let me into your heart. But will you let me into your bed?"

CHAPTER SIX

When Tres said he would take me to bed, he meant it literally. We stripped down to our unmentionables and then climbed under the sheets. He didn't make a move on me, other than his groin pressed into my backside.

What he did do was wrap his arms around me. It had been a while since I'd slept with someone. Well, since I'd slept with a man. Loren had often hopped into bed with me over the past few months. But there was nothing like having a big barrel chest at your back and that hint of manhood seeking your warmth.

Tres inhaled, his nose pressed into the back of my head. Then he let out a long, sleepy sigh.

"Really?" I said. "We're actually going to sleep?"

"I told you that I would have you begging before the next time I was inside you." His hot breath brushed the cone of my ear. "Say please."

I snorted. "Screw you."

"Not tonight." He chuckled.

His chest relaxed a moment later, but his hold on me didn't. His breathing slowed, but the warmth of his breath still blazed a trail across my neck. It felt so good that I almost reconsidered making a plea.

I fought sleep for as long as I could. But nestled inside his peaceful embrace, feeling safe and warm, I succumbed.

I hadn't had a good night's sleep since Camelot. I'd only dozed as we made our way from England and across the pond to the States. I hadn't wanted to face my nightmares. But I couldn't run any longer. My body was tired and being held made me feel guarded, and the dream came at me with gusto.

I'd told Tres that I'd been having dreams. I hadn't told him that they weren't about him.

In the dream, I moved through the darkness. My eyes adjusted quickly. A light source from somewhere that I couldn't decipher illuminated my surroundings. I couldn't tell where I was. Maybe a cave? I wasn't sure.

I saw him in the distance. He had his back

turned from me. I called out to him. I know he heard me, but he wouldn't turn to see me.

He was looking at something in the distance. The only thing that could ever distract Zane from me was his artwork. I know that in the dream, he was looking at something of beauty that he wanted to capture.

I looked past him and saw it. It was a garden, filled with colors and wonders I didn't know the words to describe. I felt drawn to its beauty too. But I didn't want to get close. I knew that to get there someone would have to die.

Zane took a step toward the garden. I reached for his arm but he was beyond my grasp. I called out to him again. This time he turned.

He was so distant. His mahogany brown eyes, which had once been so open and vibrant whenever they glanced over me, were shuttered. We stood on the edge of a cliff. I knew that one more step would send him over and he would never reach the garden.

I pleaded with him with my words, my eyes, with everything that I had. He smiled sadly. Then he shook his head.

He took a step back from me, and then another. I couldn't move. I couldn't go after him. I reached out my hand. Our fingertips met. But then he took the last step and the darkness swallowed him whole.

I screamed in my dream. In the darkness of the night, my eyes slammed open as my heart pounded in my chest. The sound of my pants and my beating heart filled my ears. I was certain the racket would wake up Tres. But it didn't. He slept peacefully beside me.

His arm was slung over my hip, his body curled into mine. His warm hand caressed my belly. I felt his lips press against my shoulder blade.

I carefully extracted myself from his embrace and padded out of the bedroom. Avoiding the floorboards that creaked, I slinked off to the third room that I hadn't shown him. With a tug of a board in the wall, I stepped into the entrance that led to the underground cave. The continuation of my research could wait no longer. I needed to figure out where that garden might be before anyone else of my kind died.

I'd had my share of nightmares over my long life. They'd always been more ominous than prophetic. I'd dreamed of the Lin Kuei as they'd hunted me. I'd been visited by the slumbering spirit of a Titan goddess warning me about the apocalyptic mischief of her demigod children. And now my nightmares turned to the demise of the man I'd loved for most of my life.

I accepted that things were over between me and Zane. But I would not let anything happen to him. Not if I could stop it, and I would.

I shut the hidden door to my cave firmly behind me. If Tres woke up in the middle of the night looking for me, he'd assume I'd gone outside and not underground.

I liked to call the underground vault my Cave of Knowledge. I'd built shelves into the rock interior. Like a wine cellar could preserve hundred-year-old bottles of wine, the airtight cave with its cool temperatures kept moisture and oxygen away from the documents and artifacts I had stored down here.

The texts were organized according to era, then culture, and finally, subject. Most were original copies; many were written by my own hand.

My first memory ever was of symbols and their meaning. I remembered a hand drawing out the symbol that had been burned into my skin. Only it had been written on something that looked like stone with a stylus that had a burning tip. I couldn't see the face of the author, but I remembered the delight when I came to recognize that the shape belonged to me. It identified who I was.

I remembered holding that fire-branding device in my hand and making other symbols. I remembered the symbols clearly today. But they were the only symbols that I didn't know the meaning of. I'd also never seen their like in any writing.

I wondered, had that all happened in a garden? Maybe one filled with angelic beings? Were they marking time, waiting for our return? And if so, why did our herd need to be culled?

Determined to find the answer, I passed by my centuries of personal diaries. I hadn't updated them in the last few decades. This last year I'd had a good number of revelations that needed to be recorded. But not now.

I bypassed my treasured collection of texts from the destroyed Library of Alexandria, which contained the original canon of the Holy Bible. The evidence I was looking for was not contained in there, as the Qumran Scrolls had already told me.

I was looking for something that I'd written down after the Bible had been written. It was a tale told to me about creation. A creation story from Mesoamerica.

As the world's first archaeologist, I'd watched so many cultures been born and erased. Before I'd dug things up, I'd written them down. I'd watched history be written, rewritten, erased, and twisted. These records, the ones written by my own hand, I knew were all true. They'd been seen firsthand or told by the ones who'd been there.

I reached up high on one of my shelves and brought down a scroll that was over a thousand years old. It had been told to me by twin brothers while I was in the highlands of what would come to be known as Guatemala.

Before Columbus sailed to the west, the Chinese, the Irish, the Africans, and likely many others had visited this land. I'd hitched a ride on a Viking expedition in the tenth century.

The natives my Viking captain, Leif Erikson, encountered in Vinland were hostile to the Norsemen. But they were very welcoming to me. I suppose because I looked more like them than the fair-skinned, hairy seamen. I stuck around after the Vikings headed back across the waters and made my way down the continent.

I spent time with many Native American tribes in North America, but the Mayans of Central America won a special place in my heart. The stela graphics that decorated their temples were much like the hieroglyphs of Egypt, though the cultures had not had any contact.

One day, a Mayan king brought me to meet two individuals he called the God Twins. The two men I was presented to were identical down to the spots on their skin. I'd assumed they were lepers, but I'd never seen a leper with black spots and in such a beautiful design all over the body. I assumed it was ritual painting. I know now that my assumption was wrong.

I sat before the twins and acted as their scribe as they told a fantastical story. Now, I opened that document and looked at my notes. I had a habit of writing in the language of the country or culture that the story was told in. This story that the God Twins had told me was written in the K'iche language.

The twins told me of their birth to an angelic mother. A daughter of Xibalba, the underworld. They said their conception was immaculate, as their father's skull spat in their mother's hand and she became pregnant in her womb.

I remember holding in my laughter as I continued to transcribe their story. I could see on the parchment where I'd fudged the symbols for the word-symbol of conception. I hadn't believed a word they'd said at the time of the telling. It wasn't my job. I only wrote down the words.

There were a couple of words that I zeroed in on now. The word for angel was one of them. The word Xibalba was another. They'd called their mother the K'iche equivalent of an Elohim. Specifically, a Seraphim. They said they'd come from the underworld of Xibalba, where there was a garden in which they played games with others of their kind.

I hadn't thought much of their story back then. But now I realized that hadn't been the only time I'd heard the tales of those twins.

The story of the God Twins was repeated up and down the continents of the Americas. In the Iroquois, they were called Teharonghyawago and Flinty Rock. In the stories of the Mohawk, they were Okwiraseh and Tawiskarun. The Mayans called them Hunahpu and Xblananque, or Hunter and Jaguar.

As the pieces began to fall together, I realized that they were all the same men. The God Twins, the Hero Twins, the Trickster Twins. They were real, living beings. They were most likely gods or angels. And, if the stories across numerous Native American cultures were to be believed, they had traveled from the underworld garden of Xibalba to the surface many times over.

I knew that because I knew their children. In fact, I was very good friends with two of their daughters. And when I made it to Guatemala to tell them that I had once met their deadbeat dads, they were gonna be pissed and claw my head off.

But I'd withstand the ire of those two Mayan queens if it got me entrance to Xibalba and the underworld of the angels.

 lay in the bed. My legs were spread-eagled, my toes touching each of the bottom corners of the mattress. My arms were flung wide, my palms up in offering. Though I was exhausted mentally and physically, the gods of sleep didn't come to take my sacrifice.

I stared up at the thatched roof I'd constructed with my own hands. The lines and swirls danced in my head, trying to form symbols. But I was too tired to decipher anything else.

I turned over on the mattress and buried my head in a pillow. Inhaling, I got a strong hit of the heady scent of frankincense. The essential oil clung to Tres's body as his natural scent. And now it permeated my bed and the outer room. I even smelled it on my own skin from where he'd held me all night and into the morning when I'd crawled back into bed.

I realized that Tres always smelled of the sweet, woody oil. Frankincense was often used in spiritual ceremonies in ancient times. Today, New Age followers swore by its therapeutic qualities of healing ailments and relieving stress. I inhaled again and caught the hint of pine mixed with lemon. I swallowed the vapors down and was reminded of licorice. But my anxiety and stress remained.

Maybe I needed a stronger hit. I rose from the bed in search of Tres. He'd risen with the sun, but I'd stayed behind, feigning sleep.

I didn't want to close my eyes again and bump into another nightmare. So I'd kept my eyes open and rested in Tres's hold while inhaling the peaceful scent of him. But when I breathed him in, more memories of the past pushed at the corners of my mind.

I didn't want any more memories today. When I remembered things, it only seemed to push Tres and me further apart. When I slept, the nightmares came and reminded me of the distance between Zane and me. Unfortunately, holding my breath and staying awake forever weren't options.

I took a deep breath and got out of bed. Leaving my home, I headed down to the spring. The day was bright and sunny on my island paradise. A light breeze trickled through the trees as I came into the clearing.

Tres's expensive travel bag sat on a rock near the waters. Mud clung to the bottom and face of the bag, obscuring the designer label. His clothing hung halfway in and halfway out.

I hesitated to look up, expecting to see Tres emerge from the waters in all his bronze glory. I lifted my gaze and was met with calm waters. Clear blue that almost mirrored the sky rippled gently across the expanse of the spring. I looked off into the horizon, wondering if Tres had swum out of the inlet. Then he broke through the surface.

Clear droplets arced around his head like a halo. But this man did not look like one of the sweet, rosy-cheeked cherubs that sat on the good side of the shoulder. No, the sun backlit him with a burnt orange glow. The smirk he wore would rival the horns of the devil in making a point.

He wiped the water from his face. It rolled down his chin and fell on his pecs. Most of the water fell from the precipice of the twin muscles there, but a few determined droplets braved the contoured maze of his abs. The journey ended at his happy trail since the water came up to his waist.

"Join me?" he said.

I took a deep breath. Even from this distance, the scent of frankincense wafted over to me. But I realized it was coming from his discarded clothing. Now that I was awake and my mind was clear, the mission that I was on rang louder than my desires.

"We should get going," I said.

Tres splashed water onto his chest. Once again, the drops clung to him for long seconds before rolling down the curved path and falling into the water. "You're kicking me out?"

"No," I said. "I just got what I came for."

Tres sank down into the water up to his chin. "Why do I feel like I've been used?"

"You haven't," I said, smiling as he floated away from me on his back. But then my face turned serious the further away from me that he got. "It's just that time is of the essence."

"Because you think two more of us will die?"

I crossed my arms over my middle and looked off into the distance. "You don't believe what Igraine saw in her vision?"

Tres dunked his head. The water rippled as he flipped his body and glided closer to me. When he resurfaced, he brushed the water from his face once more, and then he answered me.

"I've never put much stock into prophecies. When people make predictions they either have the game fixed or they often misread what they saw. The future never happens exactly the way we expect or want."

"Still," I said. "I'd rather be proactive. I don't want anyone else to get hurt."

I knew he guessed which particular anyone I was referring to. But he said nothing. He just continued to tread water.

"I was thinking you could help me," I said. "If you wanted to come along."

"Where are we headed?"

"I need to get to Guatemala. I want to talk to Skye and Skully."

"The Jaguar Queens?" He let out a low whistle and floated away from me again. "I am not their favorite person."

"That seems to be a recurring theme with you."

None of my friends got along with Tres. Demeter hadn't enjoyed Tres's company over some business with a temple. Arthur and his knights also didn't get along with Tres over something to do with a witch he'd once had a fling with. He and Zane were on the outs for obvious reasons. I wondered what he'd done to anger the Mayans. But I could guess.

"Don't tell me," I said. "You built on tribal lands?"

"You and I made a deal that we wouldn't talk about my work."

"While we're on a date. This isn't a date. It's a bath."

"We could make it a date."

Tres stood then. I'd expected the water to cover his manhood, but he'd come closer to me. The water slipped past his hips and exposed all his glory as he came to his full height.

I looked. Of course I looked. And, oh boy. I got so hot I had to rethink getting into the water. To cool off, of course.

Tres kept coming at me, that cocky grin on his face. As his grin spread, a memory crested in my mind like a wave gently pushing against the shore.

In my mind, Tres stepped off a boat. He was clothed, but barely. He walked through waters like a god coming out of the sea, his eyes fixed on me. I'd taken a step back at that time too. But I met with a warm chest. I didn't need to turn around to know that I'd stepped back into the embrace of Zane.

Zane wrapped his arms around me as Tres came nearer. Tres had said he'd wanted me the first time he'd seen me. And that first time, he'd said, had been when I was wrapped in Zane's arms.

Tres stood before me now. His face was a mask as he looked down at me, as though he were waiting for a shoe to drop. He'd worn that same look the other night as the memories started assaulting me. I hadn't noticed then, but now that he was close to me in the light of day, I noted there was worry in his brown gaze.

"Tres?"

"Hmm?"

"Why don't you just tell me whatever it is you're afraid I'll remember instead of waiting for me to remember it and get mad."

His lips quirked up in a smile. He ran a finger along my brow like he was memorizing my features before I took off running in the opposite direction. I thought the Trojan War was the big secret. Was there something else?

"It's not me," he said. "It's you. I know that look. You're thinking about him."

I opened my mouth to deny it, but my teeth got caught on the inside of my lip. Here before me stood this powerful man. He'd bared his body and soul to me. Literally. But I was still clinging to the past. The least I owed him was the truth.

"Yes," I said. "I am thinking about Zane. We argued the last time we spoke."

It had been more of a disagreement than an argument. Neither of us had raised our voices. We just stood on different sides of the issue, unwilling to cross the line or even meet in the middle.

The middle was Tres.

Zane and I had had our fair share of ups and downs in the last five hundred years together. But I'd never once strayed, never thought about it. I loved him—present tense if I was honest. There was no reason to lie to myself. The man still paid rent in my head and my heart. But I was ready to move on now.

"I'm worried about him," I said as I stood in Tres's loose hold. "He doesn't want to talk to me or see me. Because he knows I'm with you. And I am. I'm with you."

Tres's hold on my upper body tightened slightly. My palms rested against his warm skin, and I felt the beating of his heart on my palm. His torso maintained its distance. Without looking down I could tell that he was eager to take the leap, but the gap between us was still wide.

"What I was remembering just now was a time when I'd been with him but I'd felt drawn to you.

You were coming off a boat. Your eyes were kohled and you were dressed in regal clothing."

Tres nodded. "That must have been Mesopotamia."

"When?"

"Around 2700 BCE or so."

He shrugged, releasing his hold on me. He wrapped a towel around himself. He must have brought it with him, because it was luxurious. His brown skin was in stark contrast to the white terrycloth.

"2700 Mesopotamia?" I said, watching his firm backside as he slid into a pair of pants. "That was during the reign of Gilgamesh."

The Sumerian myth of the legendary king of Uruk was immortalized on a number of ancient tablets. But the seminal work was *The Epic of Gilgamesh*. I knew for a fact it wasn't written by me because it was written in poetic verse. I was far more a scientist than a romantic.

The writings about the king were fantastical with his dealings with gods and mortals alike. The great king fought demons, seduced women, built awe-inspiring works of engineering. His greatest possession was the deep, life-altering bond he had with his enemy-turned-brother, the wild man called Enkidu.

The legends told that Enkidu had been sent by the gods to tame the wild ways of the arrogant king. But Enkidu had been born of nature and was uncivilized. Until a woman—some say a prostitute, others say a priestess; in the ancient world, they were often synonymous—tamed him with her lovemaking. Once tamed, Enkidu faced off against Gilgamesh in a knock-down, drag-out brawl.

But somewhere during the fight, they found they had a lot in common, and a bromance ensued. They embarked on a road trip of adventures through the ancient world. It was the first bro story ever recorded.

"Did you know him?" I asked Tres. "Gilgamesh? And his bestie, Enkidu."

"I did." He turned from me. The same far-off look I got clouded his gaze. "So did you."

I watched Tres as he buttoned his shirt. The methodical motions of slipping a button into a hole and turning it so that it caught lulled my brain back through time.

I remembered my earlier vision of standing next to Tres as he directed the building of ziggurats. I remembered the regal clothing he wore in that vision and the one where he stepped off the boat. The pieces were falling into place.

"You? You're King Gilgamesh?"

"My one and only attempt at ruling. I was much more interested in building the city of Uruk than ruling over the people."

But that wasn't all. In my mind's eye, I turned and saw Zane coming toward us. A huge smile on his handsome face, his hair wild and his clothes slightly unkempt. But I didn't seem to care. Zane scooped me into his arms and kissed me passionately before turning to Tres and embracing him with loud claps on the back.

"And Zane..." I asked.

Tres tucked the tails of his buttoned shirt into the waistband of his pants instead of answering me. I watched as he transformed from island native to tycoon on holiday. The transformation was jarring, but not as much as the revelation.

"Wait!" I said. "Are you telling me I'm the prostitute in this story?"

Tres chuckled. Then he reached for me again. This time my hand landed on soft linen instead of wet skin. One of my nails snagged in the fabric of his business shirt.

"Prostitute, no," he said. "Priestess, enchantress,

thief? Those titles would be more like it. You stole both of our hearts."

Tres's hand swiped a tendril of hair behind my ear. He toyed with the strand a moment before meeting my gaze. His face was so open, so vulnerable. It was me that looked away this time.

"We should get going," I said.

Tres nodded. He released his hold on me. But then he captured my hand, and we walked the path back, together.

CHAPTER EIGHT

The flight was smooth as butter. It was as though the air pockets moved out of the way of the mighty Tresor Mohandis's private jet.

"Pomegranate martini?"

I turned to face the stewardess. She was a six-foot-tall blonde who I'm sure was an ex-model. I couldn't tell if she was sneering at me or if she was over-botoxed.

I'd washed up with some water from the spring and slipped back into the jeans I'd been wearing when we'd left Camelot. My shirt had been pretty ruined during the hunting debacle the previous night. I was dressed in one of Tres's business shirts.

Engulfed was more like it. Where the garment should've sat on my shoulders, the caps slipped down closer to my elbows. I'd rolled up the cuffs a couple of times and they still hung to my wrists.

The stewardess had handed the clean shirt to me. After she'd handed me not one but two too-small women's T-shirts. One was a Disney shirt gone wild. Mickey and Minnie stood side by side, but Mickey was copping a feel on Minnie's ass. The second one was red with a Santa hat. It read, "I'm on the naughty list" in bright white and green letters.

I'd tossed the shirts back at the stewardess, completely unamused by and unconvinced of her helpful hospitality. I wondered how many women she'd handed a morning-after shirt to. I wondered if she'd ever worn a morning-after shirt herself.

Finally, she'd handed me one of Tres's shirts. I'd taken the shirt, and now I took the drink. It was a pretty mean martini. That gave her points.

I stood up and wobbled a bit. Alcohol didn't typically affect Immortals the same way that it did humans. There was something about our metabolism that burned it off quickly. But if you had more than one in a short amount of time, you could get a nice buzz. This was my third since we took off.

My head was reeling from all the memories that had come at me in the span of twenty-four hours. I'd never remembered so much, so quickly, so clearly. And not so far back in time.

Zane and I had been together in ancient Mesopotamia. I didn't understand how he couldn't have told me that. Or about our time together in Greece before the Trojan War. Or about the original argument that sparked our current break-up—that we'd been together back in China. Or was it before China? Had what happened in Greece been the reason I'd run off to China?

There were so many secrets coming to light that my head was spinning. I downed the alcohol, and my knees wobbled a bit. It wasn't enough to make me feel drunk. I had to chalk it up to being in the presence of another Immortal for a week.

Had Tres and I spent that much time together? I'd met him in the midst of gunfire in Mosul. Then we'd spent a couple of days in Caerleon while Loren recovered from being sliced and diced by Yod. And then we'd spent the night on my island.

Yeah. It had been a week. And we hadn't killed one another. I called that progress in this relationship.

He'd let his guard down with me while we'd stayed on my island. As the dirt got under his nails and the scruff grew on his chin, he'd opened up to me. As the plane had taken off, he'd kept his fingers laced with mine. I'd felt the calluses of his fingertips and smiled down at the ruggedness of his once-manicured nails.

The moment the seatbelt light went off and the Wi-Fi light went on, his phone began to ring. I hadn't even realized he'd had it on him. He ignored it for the first couple of minutes, but its constant buzzing was like a gnat flitting right in front of his nose.

An assistant materialized from the recesses of the plane and tugged Tres's attention. The preppy kid spoke in an obvious code regarding business dealings. Tres gave me an apologetic grimace, an absentminded buss on the cheek, and then he rose to take the documents from the assistant and the call on the phone.

That was thirty minutes ago. Setting the martini glass aside, I took a moment to check my own cell phone. I didn't have any text messages, voice messages, or emails. I shut my phone off and wandered the plane looking for Tres. There were a lot of places for him to hide.

There was a general seating area that could easily hold a couple dozen passengers. And when I say general seating, please note that I meant that each seat was cushioned and wide in the fashion of a television recliner that leaned back with the flip-up flap for your feet. Beyond that common area, the rest of the plane looked like the inside of a luxury suite.

There was a kitchen with a refrigerator, cabinets, and a freaking dishwasher. Then there was a business area with a desk and computers—yep, plural. I bet he had his very own satellite for the Wi-Fi on this plane.

And then there was a bedroom with a full bed and a television. I stood in the doorway, staring at the fluffed pillows. The sheets were pulled straight with the comforter turned down.

We hadn't slept in here. The flight from the Caribbean to Central America was a short one, made shorter on this fast jet. But I'm sure there had been any number of women in this bed with Tres in the past. Probably even that stewardess who was generous with the vodka in those martinis.

Is that why she'd been smirking at me? Because she knew I was getting off, while she would be staying...and maybe getting off later.

Tres and I hadn't exactly defined the boundaries of our relationship. From what I knew of his past lives, and what I read about him in the magazines, I wasn't sure he believed in monogamy. Hell, he'd stolen his best friend's girl at least twice.

I, however, did believe in monogamy. Even though my past pattern of getting with this man might seem to indicate otherwise. But when I committed, I was all in.

Is that what I wanted to do now? Did I want to dive all in with Tres? Would he dive in with me? Or would he want to keep a pinky toe in this bedroom with too-small women's T-shirts?

I took a step into the bedroom. At the same time, the bathroom door opened. Tres came out of the bathroom and stepped near to the bed.

Gone was the scruff on his chin from the day in the wild. Vanished was the dirt beneath his nails from his time in the outdoors. The thick locks atop his head were tamed. His large body was clothed in an expensive business suit with a perfectly knotted tie that lay on his chest.

He was straightening out his cufflinks when he saw me in the doorway. He looked from me to the bed. Then he looked back at me with an eyebrow quirked. The way he swaggered toward me made me feel like prey; it reminded me that the suit was a lark and this man was a predator at heart, a conqueror by nature.

I held still and let him catch me. A slow smile ticked up his lips as I remained pliable in his arms.

His lips hovered above mine, and I gulped down that spicy scent of frankincense. Even though he'd bathed in the springs just hours ago, and washed off again in his shower now, it still permeated his very being, making me wonder if he was, in fact, born of the gods.

Tres nuzzled at my lips, and I sucked down a mouthful of the heady scent until it filled my lungs and clouded my brain.

"There's not enough time before we land for me to do the things I have planned for you, Theta. But I'm not in this for sex."

I pulled back to stare at him. I felt my brows raise into my hairline. Tres chuckled at my expression.

"I do plan to have some," he clarified. "A lot, in fact. With you. Soon would be nice."

"What are you waiting for?" It wasn't a come-on. I was genuinely curious as to his reasons for not tossing me down on the mattress and gaining us both entry into the mile-high club.

He ran his hands down my forearms and came to rest on my hips. I raised my arms until they came around his neck. My fingertips brushed through the soft locks of his hair. He leaned closer; the feel of his hot breath mixed with the woodsy scent of the oils that clung to him made me woozier than the altitude or the alcohol.

Memories of his touch lit the corners of my mind and I opened for him, eager to be the star of his attention once more. Before his lips touched mine, a loud knock sounded on the frame of the open door.

"Mr. Mohandis," said his assistant. "A call for you."

"Take a message," growled Tres.

"It's the President of Mexico calling."

Tres inhaled. His fingers flexed on my hip. When he sighed, he leaned in and pressed his lips briefly to mine before pulling completely away.

"This will just take a moment," he said.

It took more than a moment. We were both strapped in for landing by the time he got off the call.

Tres took my fingers in his again. "I'm sorry."

"Seems the only way I can get your full attention is in the middle of a war zone or on a desert island."

"I have one of those."

"A war zone?"

He grinned at my flippant remark. "An island. Not exactly a fortress of solitude, more a private resort. You showed me yours. Next, I'll show you mine."

Tres leaned in and captured my lips as we descended. The wheels of the plane touched the ground in a smooth landing, but his kiss was smoother. This time when the unfasten seatbelt light came on, he didn't immediately rise to see to his business affairs.

"You need to get out of here," he said when he broke the kiss. "Go play with the wild animals before I forget that I'm a gentleman."

"I used to think you were a beast."

"You have no idea, Dr. Rivers. When you get back, I'll take you someplace secluded where no one will hear you scream."

He unbuckled me and walked with me to debark from the plane. But as I took a step on the stair, he stayed behind.

"I have some business in Mexico," he said. "I'll wait for you there while you have a girls' night with the psycho twins."

"Skye and Skully are not psychotic." Aggressive? Yes. Violent? At times. But you would be too if you were two women ruling over a horde of wild beasts.

"We can plan another visit where it's meet-the-boyfriend time," said Tres.

"Did you just call yourself my boyfriend?"

"Yeah. Is that okay?"

"Yeah." But my voice wobbled, and he heard it.

"I'm a patient man, Dr. Rivers. But I'm also a ruthless conqueror."

"So what? You're going to stick a pole in…"

Tres chuckled. He pressed his lips to mine then turned and headed back into the cabin. "Tell Diaz I said *hola*, and he still owes me a case of tequila."

CHAPTER NINE

Tres let me off his jet at Carmelita Airport in El Petén, which was in the north of Guatemala. Our arrival caused quite the uproar at the tree-lined airport. I supposed that not many private jets carrying billionaire businessmen flew onto the small strip.

Scholars once called this area full of savages and a low point in human civilization. That's because those smarty-pants in breeches came to see this haven after the jungle had reclaimed it. Before nine hundred years ago, before the collapse of the Mayan way of life, Petén had been a veritable metropolis.

The powerful cities of Tikal and Calakmul were within this area. By the seventh century, the region had become the heartland of the Mayan empire, with several million people thriving within the borders, making it one of the most densely populated regions in the world at that time.

With so many great minds in one place, these cities had developed a distinctive architectural style that featured inscriptions on the monuments to the gods and rulers. These monuments and inscriptions could still be seen today. But with a massive population, over-farming became a problem and led to famine. By the time the Spanish came, they saw few towns, no roads, and overgrown jungles.

The land had remained that way for a long time afterwards and had only changed recently. As the Mohandis jet took off to the sky, I got in line for the chicken bus. A chicken bus, or *trambilla*, was a retired American school bus that had been modified by the locals with bright, bold colors to transport people, goods, and live animals. They were called chicken buses because they had a habit of cramming the three types of cargo inside, thus resembling a chicken coop.

The *ayudante* collected my money and gave me a hand up and onto the bus. In the seats were mostly young backpackers and adventurers out on a day trip, likely to the local nature park to zip line, horseback ride, and go on a safe and secure eco-adventure through the jungle canopy.

The crowded bus set into motion, bumping down the newly installed highways of the cleared jungle as the guides told stories of the ancient Mayan people. Looking out the window, I saw that many of the farmlands had been reclaimed. Not all the ancestral inhabitants of this land were happy about the modern progress. Many of the people preferred the wildness of the lands. They embraced the hot days, mild nights, and rainy seasons that brought mosquitoes out to snack on the warm-blooded. Mosquitoes didn't munch on supernatural beings. I don't think they like the way we taste.

The bus pulled to a stop at the Ixpanpajul Park and most of the tourists debarked. Though this was actually my final destination, I kept my seat. I needed to make an excursion before I headed into the wilds of the adventure park. I'd make my way back there later this evening. I had an itch I wanted to scratch in the other direction.

I rode on to Holmul. There were only a couple of individuals still on the bus along with more cargo and a number of animals. There wasn't much for tourists to do or see in Holmul. There also wasn't much interest in the ancient site for archaeologists.

But only because they didn't know what inestimable treasures they were looking at.

"Lady Six Sky was a seventh century Mayan princess who'd married into her noble title," the guide was saying now to the few tourists who remained. "She gained her power when she waged war and won a number of battles across the Mayan Empire."

"I've never heard of her," said one of the older tourists. He looked like a cross between a college professor, with his thick glasses and notebook, and an Indiana Jones cosplayer, with his ill-fitted fedora and starched khakis. "I have heard of the bloody war queen, Lady Ik' Skull from the eighth century."

The guide nodded. "Lady Ik' Skull was also known as Evening Star. She married into her power as well. But upon her husband's death, the Evening Star waged a campaign that conquered most of this territory."

Most of the stories the guide told were true. The two queens' battles here in Holmul had devastated the city and its people. But neither of them had needed a husband to rule. They had more power and command than all of the males of both of their kingdoms combined. They'd held that power at the same time, not a century apart. And they'd actually been fighting each other over a disagreement.

When Skye and Skully got pissed, especially over a family matter, everyone felt their wrath. In that particular argument, when the dust settled, the city was decimated. But before the dust had settled, the queens had made up and made peace amongst themselves. It was the last time the sisters had such a large disagreement.

I stepped off the bus at the stop in Holmul. It might be more aptly described as the middle of nowhere. Luckily, I knew exactly where I was going. This was where I'd met the God Twins and transcribed their story so long ago.

The twins hadn't only told me of their exploits underground, where they played an ancient form of basketball with a skull. They'd also told me a creation story where it had taken them three tries to make beings that were like them. I just hadn't understood that they were talking about their own children. Children I would befriend a few centuries later.

The ruins of Holmul were in the northeastern part of Petén near Belize. In its heyday, Holmul had been an important outpost with its strategic position between the Tikal and Kaanul. The ruins were mostly untouched, which was startling after the cat fight between the two sisters back in the seventh century.

I approached the monuments of Holmul. There was a ball court, funerary temples, a raised courtyard, and a burial staircase that descended to the underground. The staircase had been built by King Ajwosaj of the Kaanul dynasty. Kaanul meant "snake" in the old language. Snakes were synonymous in most Native American cultures—in fact, in most cultures the world over—with tricksters.

It was the snake that led Eve astray in the garden. The Nagas, which meant snakes, of India were the guardians of the underworld. In Norse mythology, the dragon Nidhogg would coil itself around the Tree of Life and try to choke the life out of it. And here, in the ancient Mayan culture, the Trickster Twins were often represented by snakes.

The stela on the monuments were undecipherable to modern-day archaeologists, but I'd been around when some of these were carved. I just hadn't gotten their full meaning when I was here.

The hieroglyphic-like drawings on the stela told the story of the God Twins, marking them in the form of a snake. I knew this story. I'd written it down. The stela here were far too damaged to shed any new light on the old story and provide me with any information on how to get into Xibalba, the garden where the twins dwelled. This leg of my trip was a bust.

I continued on from Holmul by foot to the nearby site of La Sufricaya. Again, I found the remnants of a ball court, the twins' favorite game that they played below ground. There were more funerary temples, and another raised courtyard was visible.

Since I'd last been here, it looked as though more destruction had happened. There had been a mound in the shape of a serpent, but that hallowed ground was now decimated. The mound had been flattened, but the site looked intentionally depressed near one of the coils. The damage looked recent. As though it had happened in the last few days.

It was possible that humans had done this. The culprits had to be either archaeologists who didn't know what they'd come across, or modern-day locals looking for something to loot.

Either way, I steamed up inside to know that the monument, an unrecoverable part of history, had been trampled. A part of human culture had been lost, never to be recovered. But also, there could have been something there for me to investigate. Something that could have saved one of my kind.

I huffed and let it go. That serpent mound wasn't the initial reason I'd come here. I came because of the writings I knew were on the walls. I went to the murals, hoping that the stela here were in better shape than the ones in Holmul.

When I came upon the monument, I found that I was in luck. The writings on the walls were still visible and intact. The hieroglyphic drawings were a mix of Mayan and Teotihuacan symbols. Teotihuacan was a settlement in Mexico.

I crouched down in the brush of the jungle and moved aside foliage to get a clearer view. The particular stela I was interested in showed calendar dates. If I could figure out when the God Twins came to the surface, I might be able to hitch a ride down to the underground by slipping in after they came out, or riding their coattails as they returned.

I found the stela I was looking for, but, staring down at it, I frowned. Mayans were known for their record-keeping. But on the stela, the days were off. The symbols weren't written in the normal style, and the mishap looked intentional.

I knew this was important, I just didn't know

how. I set about photographing the information on the stone slabs. However, the click of my camera wasn't the only sound in the deserted forest. I wasn't alone.

I turned to see a jaguar emerge from the foliage.

The beast was magnificent. The orange of his coat stood stark against the green of the jungle. An abundance of white covered his chin down to his chest. Dark spots spread across his body like a collage. But I didn't take too much time to admire the predator.

I stayed low. I wasn't sure if he was friend or foe. If he was a complete animal, or half-human and half-god.

I peered closer and noted that there was intelligence in his eyes that sparked of the supernatural. I let out a sigh. The jaguar was most likely Balam. It looked like I wasn't about to get in a wrestling match today.

"Hola, yo soy Nia, una amiga des las reinas."

It didn't seem to matter whose friend I was with this shifter. Something told me that he was likely newly born, maybe a couple of decades old or so. I hadn't been here in about a decade. So, he likely didn't know who or what I was.

Then again, my supernatural-radar might be off.

Maybe this was just an animal. Jaguars still roamed the Guatemalan countryside. With my superhuman strength, I could take a jaguar in a fight. I could do damage to a Balam, but that might piss off their matriarchs. So, just in case, I decided to try diplomacy again.

"Listen, I don't want any trouble, I'm just—"

I stopped when I heard a low growl behind me. Two jaguars? Definitely Balam. Natural jaguars were solitary creatures. The Balam were born in pairs and they stuck together, just like their tricky fathers. I didn't want to have to hurt two of Sky and Skully's siblings. But it looked like I didn't have a choice.

The first jaguar pounced. I bent my knees and jumped. Reaching my arms high, I was able to grab a tree branch. I hefted myself up into the tree. But I knew I wasn't safe. Jaguars were excellent climbers.

The second beast was already springing up the trunk and making its way out onto my branch.

Relinquishing my hold on the tree, I leaped down. I tucked and rolled but still came face to face with the first jaguar.

They were toying with me. Jaguars were apex predators, meaning they weren't the kind of meat-eaters that had anything chasing after them, save humans with guns.

I didn't have a gun. I did have supernatural strength and speed. But I was moving slowly after spending a week with Tres. I turned, preparing to run, only to meet with the second jaguar.

Once again, they left me with no choice. I put up my hands in surrender.

CHAPTER TEN

Surrendering wasn't in my nature, but I was outnumbered. Besides, I knew these shifters wouldn't kill me. At least I didn't think they would.

Jaguars were predators. But Balam, jaguar shifters, didn't hunt humans for food or sport. I'm sure I didn't smell human. Skully had told me once that I smelled like a shifter who'd taken too many baths. She'd said there was a clean smell about me that made her wrinkle her nose.

My assumption was that these shifters would take me to the destination I'd planned to head to next: Ixpanpajul National Park. Which would be better than walking there. Or calling Skully and waiting for her to come and pick me up.

I watched as one Balam shifted to human form while his brother stayed in his animal form and kept guard. The shifting process was a magic show, rolled into a contortionist's act, sprinkled with a fireworks spectacular.

It began with sparks as the animal shape called back the human form. The sparks weren't like sparkles from an American Fourth of July celebration. It was more of a lightworks show with rays of light emanating from the head and underbelly.

Hair receded from the Balam's back like moisture soaking into the body. Short, stumpy legs cracked and stretched. Claws retracted and thumbs turned inward, becoming opposable. Finally, the Balam let out a low whine. His head arched to the midday sun and his snout became a chin.

The entire process took less than five minutes. When it was done, a young man crouched on the ground in front of me. He wore only his birthday suit, which was brown, toned skin with a smattering of hair on his head, his chest, and his nether regions.

Clothes didn't shift along with bone and skin and internal organs like in the young adult books in the bookstores. When the young man stood in his human form, I didn't recognize him.

He was young. Shifters, like Immortals, stopped aging after their bodies reached a certain level of maturity. I gauged his maturity by his eyes. They were still bright and not dulled with decades or centuries of witnessing the very worst of humanity.

The other Balam, still in jaguar form, gave me a push with his nose as they corralled me into a vehicle. The naked man hopped into the driver's seat, *au naturel*, I might add. Not many traveled these roads, and if they did, they weren't likely to see that he had his balls out in the driver's seat.

The jaguar nuzzled me into the passenger seat with the tip of his canines. Once I was seated, the animal hopped into the back and breathed his hot breath down my neck.

For my part, I strapped in, slid my sunshades on, and decided to enjoy the ride. If on the off chance I was wrong and they weren't taking me to the park, I'd have recovered some of my strength and would make a better showing in the next fight. Sounded like a great plan to me.

I leaned against the headrest and snuggled into the worn seat cushions. It wasn't until I closed my eyes and slipped into a long-needed repose that I realized my mistake.

The dream began in darkness. A dark so thick

that I could rub at it with my fingertips. Then slowly, a blue light shone from somewhere deep in the cave, because I now realized that it was a cave. Illuminated stalagmites hung from the cave's ceiling and stalactites reached up from the crevices of the earth.

I felt him near. That familiar warmth shone on my back like the sun, shining brighter than the unnatural lights. I turned and Zane's chest pressed against mine. His hand was on my hip with his thumb rubbing just below my belly button; his other fingertips touched my sacrum. When I looked up at him he was so distant. His coffee-colored eyes, which had once been so open and vibrant, were closed to me.

He took a step back from me, and then another. I couldn't move. I couldn't go after him. I reached out my hand. Our fingertips met. But then he took the last step and the darkness swallowed him.

I called out his name, but the only sound that came back at me was the echo of my voice. There were beings in the distance. I couldn't make out their faces. Their bodies seemed to be made of light. The entire cave lit up, shining a pathway toward green pastures and colorful flowers of every kind.

A garden.

Zane's crumpled body lay on the grass at the entrance to the garden. The scene just beyond him was vibrant and thriving, while he lay lifeless and still. The message was clear. If I wanted to get to the garden and get to those shining beings, it was over Zane's dead body.

I jerked awake on a silent scream. My hands clenched empty air. The heels of each of my feet pressed against the floorboards of the car.

Behind me, I heard a growl and felt the sharp point of a canine. Beside me, the naked man kept his silence and his eyes on the road. The ground beneath the tires changed from smooth asphalt to graveled path.

I used the bumpy movements of the car to shake off the nightmare. As the wheels tripped over rocks, Tres's voice sounded in my mind. He'd said that he didn't put much stock into prophecies, that people often misread what they saw, and that the future never happens exactly the way it was foretold.

I knew that. I'd seen that happen many times. I was armed with the possibilities. My plan was to be proactive about changing the potential path that was set out.

Zane might not want to be a part of my life anymore, and I might still be pissed off at him for keeping so many secrets, but I would be damned if I let anything happen to him. He might not be my lover anymore, but he was still, and forever would be, my family.

In the distance, I heard the happy squeals of families as they played in the park. Up overhead, I saw adults and teens ziplining through the forest canopy. On the ground, I spotted toddlers and adolescents tossing scraps at caged wild boars. We left the safety of the amusement park behind and rounded to the back where the jungle pushed up to the back door of a large manor.

For a long time, the Balam had fought to keep humans out of their natural habitat. But modernization pushed at them. Eventually, the beasts of these forests came up with a happy medium. That was Ixpanpajul Natural Park. The park was privatized just over a decade ago and now offered adventure and ecotourism for humans out front. But around the back, the wild still prowled.

A group of naked men lounged in lawn chairs. Interspersed with them were large jaguars, napping and snacking on raw meat that looked like fresh kill. In fact, I knew it was fresh kill by the blood on the animals' muzzles. As one naked male leaned over his chair to reach for a bottled beer, I saw the red stains of blood on his fingertips.

The vehicle came to a halt at the back of the house and the driver got out. He gave me a nod, indicating that I should do the same. But as I reached for my seatbelt, I noted that my limbs felt heavy and my nose itched.

The distance from Tres and the rest in the car had done me good. But, from this strong, instant flare-up of the allergy, it was clear that another Immortal was nearby. When I was too slow in shaking both the allergic reaction and the sleep from my body, the young shifter gave me a shove.

"What the hell are you cubs doing?" came a booming growl, followed by loud stomping down the stairs from the back porch.

A wicked grin spread across my face at the sound of that deep voice. I looked up at my naked captor. The man's cocky grin slipped as he realized the booming ire was directed at him and not me. I smirked like a little sister who'd gotten another sibling in trouble. My grin also had a huge helping of *I told you so*.

"What do you think you're doing putting your hands on her?" Diaz rounded the young shifter and slapped him on the back of the head.

"She was out at Holmul and then La Sufricaya," said the kid in stuttering Spanish. His voice was high-pitched, reinforcing that I was right about his age. He rubbed the tender spot at the back of his head as he stumbled over his words. "We thought she might have been the one who destroyed the serpent mound."

Diaz's face contorted into something resembling incredulity and humor. He turned to me and pointed a thumb at them. "They thought you of all people would destroy a part of history."

I shrugged my shoulders. Yeah, it was absurd. But it was more interesting to me that the damage was, in fact, done recently and the Balam were searching out the culprits.

"Do you know who this is?" Diaz demanded.

I wanted to tell him that I'd already played that card, but Diaz had more authority than I did. Besides my head was a bit foggy and there was a crick in my neck from the allergy that rolled off his big shoulders.

"That's Beleheb," said Diaz. "My sister."

I had a lot of aliases. My name in the ancient Mayan dialect of K'iche was one of my least favorites. It made me sound like the sister of the devil.

The naked man and his brother, still in animal form, both turned their noses to me. I waved my fingers at them. The finger waggle could've been interpreted to mean *Pleased to meet you* or it could've meant *Was nice knowing you*. That depended on Diaz's mood. Like the Balam, he was protective of his family.

Diaz was the only Immortal who actually looked at us all as family. He'd even claimed Yod as his brother, believing that there was good in that psychopath. I did not look forward to breaking the news of Yod's death as well as Epsilon and Vau's passing to him.

Diaz growled at the two young shifters and they took off into the jungle.

"Sorry about that, *manita*. Those toms are still young. Only fifty years old. They just came to us last decade and are still learning our ways."

Diaz pulled me into a bear hug. He was a big guy, bigger than Tres if you can imagine that. His bronze skin was taut, pulled over muscles that strained not only his shirt but his skin. His long black hair hung down his back from a widow's peak. His grin was infectious and I couldn't help but giggle as I pulled back. Allergy aside, I'd missed him.

"You know you could've taught those brats a

lesson," he said. "They could've used an ass-kicking."

"I figured I'd give in and get a ride instead."

"That's my girl. I should've figured you'd be on your way here."

He turned us both toward the stairs to the back of the manor. I had to take two at a time to keep up with his long gait as we went into the back door. Diaz knew I stuck my nose in whenever there was destruction of an ancient site or an artifact to be unearthed. But I hadn't heard about La Sufricaya.

"How long ago did the destruction at the site happen?" I asked.

"Destruction?" He frowned. "Oh, you mean the serpent mound near Holmul. That was a couple of days ago. Anyway, you'd better hurry up. Those toms aren't the only fresh meat around here. We just got a new kitten in from the States."

A tom was the term for a male Balam. Females were called queens. But since two Balams had actually been ruling queens in this region, the shifters began using the term kitten for young girls. And by young they could mean anywhere from newly born to a hundred years old.

I wondered when and where these new kittens were born? It would help me to narrow down my search for their fathers. There weren't just shifters here in Central America. There were tribes all over the Americas, from the most northern and icy parts of Canada all the way down to the bottom of Chile.

"Where were they born?" I asked.

"They were born in North America, California to be exact. They were the spawn of an actress, a Disney princess from some television show about a mouse club? Unfortunately, only one of the kittens survived."

My heart instantly sank for the poor girl. Shifters, be they jaguars, wolves, or cougars, were not solitary creatures. They were all born in pairs and were connected to their twin sibling. I'm certain it was like having a limb cut off to be out in the world alone. My heart ached for the poor kitten.

"The Mohegan sent her here last week. Thought Skye and Skully could rear her better than they could since she was a kitten."

The Mohegan were the North American tribe of wolf shifters. If memory served me right, they hadn't had a female born in the north for over a hundred years.

"Her name is Nala," Diaz was saying as we approached Skully and Skye's home office. "She's named after some character in a picture film. But like I said, you should get in there. She's trying to sink her claws into your man."

"My man?" A prickle started up my spine. My hands went to my stomach instead of around my back as butterflies fluttered inside there. It had nothing to do with the allergy.

I knew it wasn't Tres behind the door Diaz was reaching for. Aside from the fact that Tres didn't get along with the queens, I'd seen his plane take off earlier this morning. The door to Skully's office opened and my chest tightened.

The first thing that hit me was relief. The alleviation of all my anxieties about where he was and whether or not he was okay nearly knocked me back and out of the door. But I held my ground and took him in, so happy to see him standing in the light of day and not falling through a crack in the earth.

He leaned against the back of a couch. I made out the outline of his strong shoulders beneath the linen of his shirt. His head was turned and his chin dipped down toward his shoulder. A lock of his dark, curly hair fell over his forehead, obstructing my view of his eyes. But I was used to that. Zane's hair always fell over his eyes and he'd pout like a child whenever I insisted he cut it.

He'd grown a beard since last I'd seen him months ago. He hadn't done that in decades, even though I'd begged. I loved the feel of his whiskers against my face… and other places. Plus, I'd always felt that it made the quiet, thoughtful artist look a bit dangerous.

He wore a polite smile on his face, seeming amused like he always did when women hit on him. There was a young woman speaking to him. She spoke animatedly, flipping her hair, leaning in and touching his forearm. I didn't hear a thing she said. My gaze was focused on Zane.

His brow crinkled in the way of someone who knew they were being watched. His nostrils flared, and that's when I knew he knew of my presence.

It was odd to see that he didn't have any paint under his nails, only a bit of dirt. I wanted to ask him what he was working on. I wanted to run into his arms and hold him to me. It was the longest we'd been separated in over a century.

But I didn't run to him. I held still for him like I always did. I was a good model. I could hold a pose for hours for him to draw, paint, or sculpt me.

Zane's shoulders tensed and his lips pursed. I waited with bated breath for him to turn and do a slow survey of my body, to search out a new angle to capture.

But he didn't turn toward me. He turned away from me. He gave his attention back to the little kitten mewing to be petted.

CHAPTER ELEVEN

"Bele," called Skully. "You're late."

The sun backlit Skully's shoulders, like a headdress of golden rays. It made her copper-colored skin shimmer like a treasure brought to light.

Diaz managed to fit his big body between me and the door. He made his way over to Skully and picked her six-foot frame up off the ground. Dipping her head back, he drank deeply from her mouth before setting her back on her feet.

Skully caressed a finger over Diaz's lips for just a second. But then she turned from her lover and crossed strong arms over an ample bosom. Shrewd, dark eyes found mine and glared with accusation.

"Well?" she demanded.

"I wasn't expected," I said in my defense.

Skully looked to Zane, then back at me as Diaz wrapped his arms around her from behind and nuzzled at her neck. It had been a while since I'd visited, but I remembered that the two could never keep their hands off each other for longer than a minute. In fact, I'm sure a minute was their longest record.

Zane and I had often joked about their incessant public displays of affection. On one of our many double dates over the last few centuries, there had been more than one time where they had forgotten we were in the room with them, and Zane and I had nearly been unwitting participants in an orgy.

"We're not together," said Zane.

They were just three little words. They were true words. But they punched me in the gut just the same.

His back was to me. His fingers gripped the top of the couch he leaned against. He still had yet to turn and even acknowledge my presence.

Both Diaz and Skully turned back to me as a unit. Diaz's brows were raised in surprise. Skully's were narrowed in annoyance.

"You left him again?" she said.

"No." I lifted my chin. "He left me."

Silence filled the room as my words reverberated off the wood paneling and then sank down to the cold stone floor. We were speaking in English, but it felt as though my words were lost in translation to the couple. They looked from me to Zane, and then to each other, trying to puzzle out my meaning.

"Awkward," sang the little kitten as her finger traced a path from the top of Zane's shoulder down his bicep.

Zane didn't move out of her clutches. He had no reason to, other than the fact that she was a child. She looked to be eighteen, but I knew she had a couple of decades. Still, a relationship with her would be like robbing the cradle for someone Zane's age.

"Hello, Zane," I said.

He turned, just slightly. When he did, the little kitten's claw snagged the cuff of his shirt sleeves. I couldn't take my eyes off her pink fingernail trapped in the cotton of his shirt.

"*Bonjour*, chicken livers."

My gaze snapped up to Zane's. My mouth fell open. It was a struggle to shut my lips in order to get the words to form. "What did you just call me?"

Zane quirked an eyebrow. "Your name. Unless you've changed it again?"

I gave a little shake of my head. My mind rewound the last couple of seconds, when my attention had been focused on Nala's fingernail and not Zane's words. What he'd actually called me was Dr. Rivers.

He never called me that. He never called me anything but Nova or *mon coeur*. But I suppose he wouldn't be calling me those pet names anymore. He would no longer be petting me. I was no longer in his heart.

"I didn't know you were going to be here," I said. And then, for some reason, I tacked on the muttered phrase, "Since your phone seems to be malfunctioning."

"My phone works just fine." His tone was brisk. His brown eyes were dormant, like a piece of plywood.

I glared at him. But he still wouldn't meet my gaze. He turned his face away from me and tilted his head up toward the other side of the room, where a breeze blew in through the open window. He took a deep, labored breath.

"You know," Nala stage-whispered, "I've had my fair share of stalkers, too. Best thing to do is to not give them any hope. Just cut them at the knees with the truth."

The little vixen turned to me with a smile that Cruella de Vil would've cowered from. She leaned her perky little B-cups against Zane's forearm and wrapped her fingers around his bicep. She might as well have lifted her leg and let out a stream of urine on him. She was clearly trying to mark her territory.

I didn't see red. I saw crimson. Running down her cute little button nose. But a strong hand wrapped around my bicep.

Diaz.

How the heck had he gotten to me so quickly. I hadn't even seen him move. I could break his hold. His grip was only a hurdle. I could jump it if I wanted. The amused grin on his face told me he'd let me go if I did try. Diaz was used to territorial spats from living in a compound filled with shifters. More so because he had the Queen B on his arm.

"Nala," Skully snapped.

Nala straightened. It wasn't the immediate snap to attention that one of the male Balam would give to their queen. Nala's insolence reminded me that the kitten was new here. She'd learn soon enough.

"This is my guest," said Skully. "Bele has been a part of this family for centuries and you will treat her with respect."

"I respect my elders." Nala smiled sweetly. "I

have manners. Why don't I get you a glass of wine, Zane?"

Zane looked down at her. He offered her a smile. It wasn't his polite smile that said *thanks, but I'm not interested*. It was something I hadn't seen before.

Zane released his hold on the couch and placed his hand at the small of her back. They walked past me, actually veering over to the far side of the room out of my path. I turned and watched them go. Actually, my gaze stayed on Zane's fingers at Nala's lower back.

"I'll go with them," said Diaz. "Make sure she doesn't get into trouble."

He winked at Skully as he went out the door. Skully blew him a kiss. The door closed and my shoulders slumped from having to hold my head high for so long.

"Trouble in paradise?" asked Skully.

"What?"

I stared at the closed door and chewed at my lower lip. He hadn't looked at me. He hadn't touched me. He'd barely spoken to me.

But that was his prerogative. He could be angry and hurt, as long as he did it alive. And preferably not with that little alley cat.

"No," I said, turning to Skully. "We're cool. It was mutual. We said we'd remain friends."

I'd said that. Zane had asked me to give him space. I had called him a week ago to check on him. But I'd had a reason for that. An Immortal had just died and two more were prophesized to kick the can. I had to make sure it wasn't him.

Okay, so, I may have texted him a couple of times since then. Perhaps as recently as today. But just to make sure he was okay. I wasn't trying to get back with him.

"I'm seeing someone new," I said.

"You're dating a human?" Skully wrinkled her nose. "What's the point in that besides scratching an itch?"

Skully was the type of girlfriend who didn't beat around the bush. She would tell you if your butt looked big in those jeans. She would tell you if your fashion sense was out of whack. She would tell you when you were being an idiot.

I opened my mouth to correct her that the man I was seeing wasn't a human. And then I promptly closed my mouth. None of my girlfriends liked the new guy I was dating. Demeter didn't get along with Tres. Skully had never liked him, mainly because of the stories I'd told her about his land-grubbing ways in the past. Loren, on the other hand, was Team Broody Billionaire all the way, but for all the wrong reasons. Tres was Loren's pick for a billion reasons.

I decided not to bring him up now. Skully and I could talk about my love life later. I needed to get down to business. Before I could, Skully came around the desk and enveloped me in a bear hug, really a jaguar hug.

She had the upper body strength of a huge cat, though her shape was soft and feline. I swear her skin felt as soft as the down of a cat. I wanted to rub my head against it and seek her comfort.

"So if you're not here for him," she said when she pulled back, a huge, cat-wide grin on her pretty face, "is this a girls' trip?"

"I wish it were only that. I'm looking for your fathers."

"You and about a hundred other Balam, Mohegan, and Bex."

The Bexookee were the Canadian tribe of cougar shifters. The God Twins were busy boys who didn't stay in one place. Though they didn't venture outside of the Americas, and they seemed only to care for women of Indian descent.

But the gods never stuck around to raise their kids. They had their fun with the women they chose when they came to the surface, but stuck around for a couple of days at most. Then they disappeared back underground, leaving the human women to raise their supernatural children.

They weren't big on visitation either. Their shifter children never saw the twins. Shifters grew up not understanding who or what they were. As their human families died off from old age, they eventually found others like them who would show them a different way of life. The Balam queens and their haven at Ixpanpajul Park was one of a few safe places for shifters to live both their human and animal lives without fear.

"What do you want with those deadbeats?" Skully asked.

"I think your dads might know where I come from," I said. "And if I can catch them coming above the ground or going back below, I might be able to go home."

CHAPTER TWELVE

When the conquistadors arrived in this new-to-them world, they looked up at the pyramids and temples, they looked out at the brown people and their sophisticated social structures, they looked down at the hieroglyphic writing that had evolved before theirs, and they burned as much of it to the ground as they could to hide the evidence.

Luckily, for humanity's sake, I was a hoarder. I'd written down much of the history and tales of this world before it was new to Europeans. Many of those manuscripts were stored on my island. I pulled out the document from a millennium ago and unrolled it onto Skully's desk.

"You met my fathers?" She didn't look down at

the *Popol Vuh*. She glared at me; betrayal was flint in her hard gaze.

I held up my hands. "I forgot."

Skully squinted her eyes and I swore they sparked, as though she was ready to shift into animal form. Instead of altering her shape, she cocked a hand on her hip.

"What?" I mirrored her motions. "Do you clearly remember everyone you've met and had a conversation with from the last thousand years?"

"Humans? No. Shifters and other supernatural creatures? Yes. Two twins claiming to be gods? Oh, I'd definitely remember them."

"Well, I just remembered."

Skully rolled her eyes, but before she could launch into me anymore, the door to her office flung open and her mirror image appeared in the frame.

All shifters were completely identical physically, in both animal and human form. They could tell each other apart by smell. But for those of us with normal olfactory senses, the only way to tell them apart was by their personality.

Shifter twins were usually opposites. Not like black and white or fire and water. They were divergent like the Chinese representation of yin and yang. Their differences were more complementary than opposing.

Where Skully was dressed in dark fatigues and a tank top, her sister Skye wore a pastel-colored skirt and a silk top. Skully's face was set in a permanent smirk with a calculating gaze, whereas Skye smiled slyly but her eyes were fox-wide with cunning.

Skully looked like the one ready for a fight. But I didn't fail to note the blood on Skye's top as she came at me with open arms.

"Bele!"

The blood was warm on her chest and I felt it seep into my skin as she embraced me. I didn't doubt for a second that it wasn't hers. Skye pulled away from me and looked me over.

"I just came from teaching those two toms who accosted you a lesson. But it doesn't look like they did any damage." She turned me bodily from the left to the right. Then she brought me back front and center and shrugged. "I may have been a bit too rough for the situation, but it was a good lesson for them to learn."

Skye came over to the desk and nearly sat her pasteled bum down on the document. I got to the ancient parchment just in time, bringing it up to my chest right before I remembered the blood that had transferred from Skye onto my shirt. Well, onto Tres's shirt. Neither of them had noted that I was dressed in a man's business shirt.

"I hear you and Zane are on a break again," said Skye.

"We're not on a *break*," I emphasized. "We *broke* up."

Skye waved away my words and their emphasis. "Great, then you can come on the prowl with me tonight. Have a little fun. Let down your hair a little until you two kiss and make up."

I sighed and waited for her to finish planning our night out. I knew there was no sense in wasting my breath with the facts of the matter.

Like I've said before, Zane and I had our fair share of arguments in the past. A few of them happened while we were in Balam territory. The queens were used to our spats. In fact, they worried when we weren't fighting.

For the Balam, that was how you showed affection. Hence the blood on Skye's top. Fighting made you stronger. If you didn't deem a loved one worthy of a fight, it meant you didn't care about their well-being.

So of course the queens would assume that this was just another spat between Zane and me. And at the end of it, we'd come back together, stronger than before. I was used to hearing it from Skully, who'd been with Diaz for longer than I'd been with Zane this last time around. But since her one and only marriage to a ruthless Mayan king, Skye avoided commitment like it was the plague.

"There's this bar," Skye was saying. "Lots of human men to pick our teeth with."

"Bele here just told me she remembers meeting the deadbeats," said Skully.

That got Skye's attention and effectively changed the topic. "What? Did they hit on you?"

"No, they didn't. They wanted me to record their story."

"Their story?" said Skye. "You mean of producing the world's greatest offspring and then leaving them to the wild?"

Skye was fiercely protective of her shifter brothers and sisters. That is, when she wasn't beating the crap out of them.

"But you know, it would've been nice for them to come and have a conversation with one of us," said Skully. "Tell their daughters their story. Take a moment to watch as we conquered the whole of Central America. But no, they were too busy splitting virginal thighs."

"Why would you want to meet them?" said Skye. "It's not like they can claim credit for any of our accomplishments."

"Damn right," sneered Skully.

"So, what do you want with them anyway?" said Skye.

I laid the document down on the desk again. "This is the *Popol Vuh*," I began. "It means—"

"We know what it means," Skye said, speaking for both her and her sister. Balam twins often used the pronoun *we* instead of *I*. It took a minute to get used to.

"We thought it was a fake made by a Spanish priest," said Skully.

Francisco Ximenez was a Dominican priest who was reported to have copied the current rendition of the *Popol Vuh* that was on display at a university in Guatemala City.

"He made a copy," I said. "I wrote the original. This is it."

They both peered down. In tandem, their heads tilted to the right and then the left. Even their pupils moved at the same speed as they glanced over the writings.

"This looks like gibberish," said Skully.

That's because it mostly was. The God Twins had

told me a creation story that was much like many of the creation stories the world over. But instead of coming from the stars, they said that when they came to this world it was from the core of the planet. They rose up from the earth to an empty sky and a calm sea and into the light. When they did, the waters receded and the mountains rose and they set about making the earth fruitful.

"They told the story out of order," I said, pointing at various places in the document where the parts should connect. "They had short attention spans. They talk here about how the world was created. Over here about how they created life. And here's a bit about cosmology. And finally, here is what's most important to me: their time in the underworld."

"What about this part?" Skully pointed to a hieroglyph in the center of the page. "Is this part about us? About the Balam?"

In that section, the brothers told of their three attempts at trying to create man. They said they first created the animals, and then they went about creating mankind to worship the two of them as their gods. Their first attempt at creating humans was to make them of the earth. But that creation soaked up the water and dissolved. Their next attempt was to make mankind out of wood. But those wooden creatures had no souls. Those beings they said they washed out with a flood. But finally, in the third attempt, they created man with a soul and set them about worshiping them.

"But the animals?" said Skully. "Their first creation, is that us?"

"I don't know? I didn't know that shifters existed at that time. I didn't believe the stories that they told me."

I'd recorded their story even though I didn't believe them. I'd kept it because something they said resonated with me. Something felt different about them, but I couldn't put my finger on it at the time.

"I remember they looked like regular men. With spots. But I thought those were decorative. It was the story of the underground garden where they played ball that made me remember them."

"And you think you can find them now?" asked Skully.

"There are calendar references here," I said. "You've thought before that they surface during certain astronomical events like the eclipse."

"Yes, but the problem is that the locations they pop up at have no discernible pattern," said Skye.

"I'm sure they're trying to avoid their

responsibilities, the deadbeats," said Skully. "We've been stuck raising their brats for centuries."

She spat the word *brats*, but her vehemence only told me that she loved every one of her siblings and would die for them. Like I said, violence was the Balam love language.

Skye looked at me with those cunning fox eyes of hers. "You think you know where they'll show up next?"

"I think I have a way to narrow it down. I went to Holmul to look at the stelas for dates, but they were all too damaged. I need to go to Chichén and have a look around the observatory. Will you help me?"

CHAPTER THIRTEEN

I came out of the meeting with the queens, and as soon as I crossed the threshold, I felt the tingle in my throat. I brushed my hands through my hair, then swiped my thumb over my lips, even though any lip gloss was long melted off in the heat of the jungle. Knowing my body was on display, I turned slowly, straightening my back, which touted my ass and perked up my boobs. But when my head got round to the other side, my shoulders slumped.

"Hey, *manita*."

I cleared my throat, pushing through my disappointment. "Hey, Diaz."

I peered over his shoulder, but the hall was empty. Further in the distance I saw men's bare-chested bodies moving outside. The chests were all a warmly-roasted umber and not a tan olive that spoke of the Mediterranean.

"He's up on the roof," said Diaz. "What did he do to get put in the doghouse?"

"He dumped her this time," said Skully, coming up behind me from the office with Skye at her heels.

Diaz came off the wall he was leaning against and scooped Skully up into an embrace. Skye and Skully were identical. Completely identical. But Diaz never had any trouble telling the women apart. I wondered if he'd learned to pick up their scent like the other shifters?

Skye never played any of those switching-places tricks that you heard of twins playing. She looked at Diaz as one of her shifter brothers. There was no carnal activity between male and female shifters since they all shared the same DNA from their fathers. In any case, Skye preferred to toy with lesser, mortal men.

"Really?" Diaz's tone was full of wonderment at Skully's announcement of me being the dumpee this time around. "You know I love you, *manita*, but that man has put up with a lot for you."

My head jerked back as though he'd slapped me with an open hand. But on either side of him, my girlfriends of hundreds of years nodded their heads in agreement.

"He put up with stuff from me?" I said. "Like what?"

"You're gone for long stretches at a time," said Skully. "That's murder on a long-distance relationship."

"We're allergic to each other," I said in my defense.

"You're constantly putting yourself in dangerous situations that can get you killed," said Skye.

"Hello," I said. "I'm Immortal."

"You never let him put a ring on it," said Diaz, his fingers entwined with Skully's down to where their gold bands met.

"He never wanted..." I tripped on the end of the sentence, uncertainty coating my tongue. He'd never said anything about marriage. We'd never discussed it.

"But he put up with all of that." Diaz shrugged. "I can't fathom what else she could've done to piss him off. Unless she's been hanging around Horus."

Diaz still called Tres by his Egyptian moniker. I barely remembered any of us in Egypt, but the drawings on the wall of a one-eyed, winged god were clearly renditions of Tres. I'd always pretended not to notice that Set, the god of chaos, had an uncanny resemblance to Zane.

I came back to the present to see that all eyes had made a slow migration to me in the silence. When I didn't respond to deny that I was seeing Tres, Diaz let out a long sigh. Skully and Skye shook their heads in tandem, like disappointed parents.

A couple hundred years ago, Tres had come to Central America looking to develop some of the lands that had been reclaimed by the jungle. Though the territory had been untouched for centuries, it was still sacred to the descendants of the Maya. Since money spoke louder than heritage, construction went underway and the protests were silenced. The construction brought prosperity to many Guatemalans and raised the standard of living for most. But that couldn't replace the lost history and lands that the development took away.

Skye and Skully had never forgiven him, even though Diaz had tried to bridge a peace. Zane had remained mute in the dispute. I'd stood firmly on the side of Skye and Skully back then.

"It's still new," I said in reference to my relationship with Tres.

The queens tilted their heads to the side and looked me up and down as though they were seeing me anew. Skye started at my head and moved down, while Skully started at my booted feet and moved up. I fidgeted in Tres's shirt.

"He's changed," I insisted, but then decided to change tactics since that wasn't entirely true. "I've gotten to know him better. He's not the callous villain we once thought he was."

I looked to Diaz for help. His gaze was sympathetic, but he didn't come to my aid. This was a battle he'd fought and lost centuries ago.

"You know," said Skully, "I wouldn't be surprised if he was behind the mound damage at La Sufricaya. He was sniffing around that land a few years ago."

"Didn't Zane help build those monuments?" said Skye.

"He did?" I asked, trying to pull up any recollection of that time period.

"You Immortals and your cursed memories," said Skye. "How do you all stand it?"

"We remember the important stuff," said Diaz as he gazed down at Skully.

That was true. The things that mattered most to us were easier to hold onto. But trying to hold onto thousands of years of history in the confines of a fifteen-centimeter-wide container that was the brain was completely impossible, even for a superhuman.

"You think Tres would destroy a monument that Zane built?" I asked.

"He's destroyed your relationship, hasn't he?" said Skully.

"No," I said. "That was Zane. He kept things from me. Things I'd forgotten about."

"That sounds really lame," said Skully. Behind her, Diaz shrugged in agreement. "And beyond his control if you're the one who forgot about them."

"I wish this one would forget some things," said Diaz. "But she has a memory like an elephant."

Skully punched at his forearm. "Did you just call me an elephant?"

Diaz reached for her and got a hand on her forearm. The two tussled, bumping against the wall in their grappling. Finally, Skully got loose.

Diaz bounced on his toes, his big body appearing light as he faced off with the feline. "Don't make me chase you."

"You can't catch me," Skully teased, and took off down the hall.

Diaz gave chase.

"You gonna come hunting with us?" asked Skye, ignoring her sister and her lover. "Or you got your sights set on some other prey?"

"It's over between us," I said. "Romantically. We keep trying and it's not working."

"But you're headed up there anyway."

I looked to the stairs that led to the upper part of the manse. "He's my family."

Skye nodded at that. She gave me a pat on the shoulder and then headed out the door to join her family in the daily ritual of grocery shopping, also known as hunting in the wild for dinner.

I climbed the stairs. Each step creaked in protest of my weight. But I felt light as I climbed higher. It had been days since I'd heard from him. Weeks since I'd seen him. I was just so relieved that he was alive and well.

I could've left it at that. I could've given him the space he had asked me for, and so clearly wanted to keep between us. But I couldn't be near him and not speak to him, not check in on him at the very least. It was the decent thing to do between family members.

Before I came out onto the balcony I heard the *scritch-scritch* of pencil to parchment. We were up high, but I still couldn't see the sky above the treetops. A sea of green greeted my eyes along with the sounds of Zane's artwork.

He sat on a stool, an easel before him. A jaguar

was taking shape in shades of gray lead. He looked up and away from his drawing, but not at me.

On a tree branch below lounged a jaguar. Her body was splayed out in the midst of the tree leaves in such a way that an artist couldn't help but want to capture it. I knew it was Nala for two reasons. She was alone. And her spots were so dark and close together that she looked more like a panther than a jaguar.

Skye and Skully's spots were that dark as well. It seemed to be a trait of female shifters. Female wolves and cougars had darker pelts than the males as well.

I watched Zane trace the curve of her feline form. I watched the care he took with the slope of her muzzle. By the time he began the careful shading of the detail of her tail, and he still hadn't acknowledged my presence, I couldn't hold my tongue any longer.

"I didn't know you were here." My tone was harsher than I'd meant it to be.

He said nothing. He continued his sketching. Leaning in close, he worked over a mistake in the detail. Zane never erased any of his work, feeling even the mistakes had a purpose in his creations.

I was used to his inattentiveness when he was

working. It was just that he was usually working on a piece that depicted me. I came nearer to him, only a few steps. A breeze blew at my back, causing a few loose strands of my hair to fly in my face.

Zane's fingers paused in their motion. His shoulders stiffened and he turned further away from me.

"Zane, I know I'm not doing a good job with this whole distance and space thing."

I took another step, coming up to his back. He clenched his fingers and shut his eyes. Pausing, he took a deep, labored breath.

I reached for his shoulder. Before my fingers could make contact, he shot out of his seat. The pencil he'd been using clattered to the ground, making a mark, a single point on the paved ground of the rooftop. Zane leaned over the railing. I pulled my hand back to my heart.

"If the prophecy is true, then two more of our kind could die. I just need to know you're okay. Can't we compromise?"

"Compromise?" His voice was so quiet I barely heard it. "You haven't done a single thing I've asked of you."

"I'd do better if you would answer a text every once in a while."

"You don't text every once in a while, Nia."

I jerked back. I couldn't remember a time when he called me by that name. But when he said it just now it sounded as though he spat the three letters on the ground.

"You've been texting me nearly every day, like a psycho ex-girlfriend. I come home each night expecting to find a boiling bunny on the stove."

In another life, in another time, I would've gotten a laugh out of the movie reference. But right now I was more worried about the possibility of him being a fatality.

"That's not me being psychotic," I said. "It's anxiety. I just need to know you're safe."

"I don't want to talk to you, Nia."

His words hurt, but I gasped at the impact of those two syllables: *knee-ah*. It was an assault on my ears each time he called me by my name. It grated on my nerves, like a nail scraping across my chest. I wanted to tell him to stop. To remind him that I was his Nova, his very *coeur*. But that wasn't the truth any longer. I'd relinquished both of those titles.

"If you're concerned about my welfare," he continued, "you can check in with Diaz or Delta. I keep in contact with them."

"Fine." I tilted my chin up, even though he still

was turned away from me. "Or maybe I can become Snapchat friends with the little lion queen over there."

"Here we go." He turned completely away from me now, giving me his back.

"What?" I threw up my hands. "If you want to dally with a cub, it's not my business."

"No. It's not."

I balled my hands into fists and dropped them down to my sides. "I'm just looking out for your well-being because I care about you."

"Clearly." He let out an exaggerated sigh. "As you've shown with your incessant text messages, voicemails, and emails, my desire to be left alone means a great deal to you. I gather Tresor isn't keeping you properly occupied."

"Don't bring him into it. I'm not flaunting my new relationship in your face. You're the one trying to make me jealous by chasing after some tail right under my nose."

Zane turned to look at me now. His dark eyes blazed. His voice, when he spoke, was deathly quiet. His words came out loud and clear, slow and enunciated with no trace of an accent. "You have no right to be jealous. I have never lain with another woman. Ever."

I snorted. Before this he'd only been keeping things from me. Now he was adding outright lying to his list of transgressions.

Zane stood before me. Anger radiated off his body in the late afternoon heat. He glared at me, remaining mute.

My throat felt dry. It began closing up as my heartbeat accelerated. A low crack emanated from somewhere deep inside as I tried to take in air as realization dawned.

Here's the thing about me and Zane. We argued a lot in our five-hundred-year relationship. We were a pretty normal couple after you looked past the extraordinary amount of time we'd remained together. During these many and varied arguments, Zane would let me have it when I stood clearly in the wrong. Other times, he'd smile sheepishly and bring me into an embrace when I'd proven my side of an argument was the right viewpoint. When we were both unsure but passionate about our stance, we could go at it for days, and then go at it a different way during the nights. When we were both unsure about our stance, but interested in a topic or cause, we'd talk it out, weighing every side we could see and coming to a mutually shared conclusion.

Then there were the times when Zane knew,

without a shadow of a doubt, that he was irrefutably right. Those times, he didn't bother to argue. He'd stand patiently by as I exhausted myself, trying to prove the world was flat.

Don't judge. It was a different world back then. I looked to the ground for clues. Zane looked up to the sky for facts. Along with the great astronomers of old who'd proved the curvature of the earth, Zane loved to watch the stars and draw the constellations.

There were no stars in sight. Zane stood still now, his back against the balcony. His fingers clenching the railing as though he needed it to hold him still as the world tilted. His jaw set a firm line and his mouth closed tight.

Any words I could come up with deflated as I looked at his resolve. A chill rose up in my heart and went down my spine at the clarity in his glare. At the pain weighing down his brow. At the hurt in the crinkle of his eyes.

"You know it's true," he said simply.

And I did. I'd never thought about it, but I knew he was telling me the truth. He'd been faithful to me his entire existence.

"Three thousand years." His gaze stayed focused on me as he shook his head slowly. "My faith has been unshakeable in one single truth: you. You were my purpose. You were my destiny. The reason for my very existence."

I took a step toward him. He turned away, giving me his back once more, and leaned over the railing. He took another series of deep breaths as his knuckles went white from gripping the railing.

"Zane?" I reached out a hand, but he stepped to the side just out of my reach. "Zane, please—"

He whipped around. Fast. Before I could blink, he'd backed me up against the railing. I was trapped between his arms and thin air. His nose was less than an inch from me. His eyes bored into mine.

In another time, in another life, I would have expected him to kiss me. He was close enough. But there was no desire in his eyes, not a single flicker of passion.

My heart beat loud as I stood trapped. My instincts were to run. But this was Zane. I'd loved this man for longer than I could remember. I knew he'd never hurt me physically. Emotionally? Well, that was another story.

"When I lived in Uruk," he began, "there was a tree that grew the most potent sap. It was said to be the tree of the Goddess Inanna. But Inanna wasn't a goddess. She was a witch with an unfortunate deformity that made her less than attractive. Inanna wanted to bed the king of Gilgamesh more than anything. But the king rebuffed her advances. Until he saw her tree. You see, Gilgamesh liked to bathe in the nectar of the Huluppu tree, said it cleared his mind and helped him work out engineering problems."

I swallowed, remembering bits and pieces of this ancient tale from *The Epic of Gilgamesh*. I knew now that Gilgamesh was Tres, the builder king. I was standing before his wildman of a best friend, Enkidu. After they'd fought and become friends, Gilgamesh and Enkidu went on many adventures together. The Myth of the Huluppu Tree was one such adventure.

"I see you remember this story," said Zane. "So, you two talked about me."

I opened my mouth—to say what, I don't know. But I didn't get the chance. Zane spoke over me, continuing his tale.

"Gilgamesh devised a plan where he'd seduce Inanna and I'd get the tree," Zane continued, his hot breath licking at my upper lip. "Little did either of us know that Inanna had a hell beast guarding it. He got his wick wet while I got bit in the ass, which, in a nutshell, is the story of our friendship."

Zane took another deep inhale, as though he

were using his sense of smell to wipe out any old memories of me and replace them with this new one. His eyes blazed down at me. For just a second, his guard slipped, and the pain I saw there made my knees buckle.

"He's all over you," Zane said.

I had to gulp a few times to push air down my lungs so that I could speak. Tres's shirt itched against my skin. I wanted to pull it off and over my head. "We haven't—"

"Spare me the details," Zane said, pushing away from me. "Just give me space to breathe. Please."

He took a few more steps away from me. I wanted to reach out, but I couldn't. It was the worst form of torture. No matter what I said, no matter what I did, it would hurt this man that I loved. Just because we weren't together anymore didn't mean that I loved him any less.

And since I did love him, I did the only thing I could that would bring him peace. I turned and picked up the pencil that had fallen to the ground. I put it back on his easel. Then I walked away from him.

CHAPTER FOURTEEN

The fronds and brush and vines of the jungle rushed past me as I ran. My legs pumped faster than my heartbeats. I ran so fast that I outpaced my thoughts, leaving them behind me in the dust at my heels. My emotions lightened the faster I went, and my feelings went into the wind.

The past could not catch up to me. It was a glacier that melted slowly over time, with small chunks breaking off and splashing down in the recesses of my mind. Sometimes what broke off and rose to the surface was a little too heavy, nearly pulling me under. But not today. Today, I ran from it all.

I ran so fast I saw spots. Two of the Balam ran

alongside me. It was the two males who had accosted me in Holmul.

It wasn't that I could recognize them now. Though I had noted that their coats were more orange than yellow, where the dozen other male twins were lighter and darker shades. I recognized them because I'd watched these two shift and I'd taken off running alongside them.

The three of us were after a deer that ran free in the restricted areas of the park. The antlered animal shot across my line of sight. It was fast and its movements were focused as it ran for its life. But it was on its own, and there were three supernatural predators on its tracks.

Like I'd said before, jaguars in nature lived solitary lives unless mating or caring for young. But Balam weren't born alone and they weren't fertile. All they had were each other. Their twin was their constant companion in this life.

The word jaguar came from the Native American word *yaguar*, which meant "he who kills with one leap." And that's what the twin males did. One of the Balam leaped into the air on his powerful thighs. He caught the deer by the head and then chomped down to make the kill.

I heard the crunch of bones. It didn't turn my stomach. It made me bloodthirsty.

There wasn't much for me to do as the two Balam worked together until the deer was motionless. Then they hauled their kill back to the house. I turned, looking for my own personal prey to hunt.

Most of the Balam were in the water. Fishing was a serious pastime for both natural jaguars and their supernatural cousins. Their speed and stealth made them natural hunters on land as well as in water. I watched as a shifter dipped its short tail into the water like a fishing line. This wasn't a maneuver created by the shifters; natural jaguars did this technique as well.

I had nothing for a fish to grab onto, so I turned to smaller mammals. I headed away from the water and back into the dense foliage.

The forest was filled with predators and prey. But only here in Central and South America did jaguars still roam free. They'd mostly gone extinct in North America in the 1900s. You could still find some in Arizona, but they were all natural animals, not Balam. Except for Nala.

She was the last Balam to be born on North American soil in the past few centuries. The shifters of North America were wolves. They lived as humans and hid their identity.

In the States, the Mohegan had day jobs, checking accounts, and pensions. Here at this resort, the Balam lived mostly wild lives. They woke up, played, hunted, took a nap, ate, and then went to bed only to do it all again the next day.

I had to admit, down here in the south was the life. I'd love to live a life of leisure. But nope, I had a genocidal prophecy to solve and very little cooperation or support amongst my kind to do so.

A rabbit jumped into my sight, rerouting my attention. Its bushy tail was a blur, but my sharp gaze brought it into focus. I gave chase.

It zigged and zagged as bunnies did. I zipped through the forest, ducking under branches and leaping over bushes. Still, it stayed a paw ahead of me.

My heart slammed against my chest as I pumped my legs in pursuit. Though it was trying hard to evade me, its movements were predictable. Even though it was going at top speeds, I saw its hind foot turn to the right and its body followed. Staying a hair behind, I allowed it to evade my grasp time and again.

I knew that I crowded its space and gave it little

room to breathe. I kept it in my sights, keeping on its trail, hunting it down. But couldn't it see that there were dangers out in this jungle far more lethal than me?

I was only trying to help. But would the bouncing creep let me? No. It ran until it was cornered between me and a boulder. Its steps faltered, and that's when I snatched it up with my bare hands and snapped its neck.

I made my way back to the manor, the rabbit dangling over my shoulder. There was blood on my hands. I felt a little high as I tossed my kill onto the pile with the rest of the downed prey.

In nature, jaguars didn't share their kills. But each of the twins brought their "groceries" back to the house. They piled up the kills in the backyard that led to the kitchens. I was thankful that they were going to cook the meat instead of eating it raw. I knew that wasn't just for my sake. They would eat it raw if they were out in the wild. But they were civilized. So to speak.

One by one, the Balam males shifted back to their human form. Only Diaz and I stood in clothing. Even Skye walked around with her breasts out and her Brazilian wax on display. None of the men looked. They were her brothers and she was older than all of them by centuries, though she didn't look a day over twenty-five.

Skully kissed Diaz with blood on her lips from her kill. Diaz laughed as he licked it off. I watched after them as they walked into the house. A few shifters stayed behind. Some stayed in their animal form and climbed up onto tree limbs, preparing for a short siesta before dinner.

I looked up to the tree where I'd last seen Nala. She was no longer lounging there. I couldn't stop myself. Taking a deep, cleansing breath, I turned toward the balcony.

Sure enough, she was up there. I saw her naked ass and perky breasts as she lounged on the railing. Zane caught my gaze as his pencils moved on the parchment. He didn't hold my gaze, not even for a second. He turned his attention back to his model and lost himself in his sketching.

CHAPTER FIFTEEN

The dining room was raucous. Not surprising since it was filled with two dozen shifters. Thankfully, they were all clothed for the evening meal.

There was a hierarchy to this culture. The youngest Balam sat at the foot of the long table, with the older males sitting closer to the top. Women were at the top. Skully and Skye sat at the head of the table in chairs next to each other.

It wasn't that Balam were a matriarchal society. It was more that Skye and Skully were the oldest Balam and the strongest. The two had at one point conquered and ruled much of the Mayan world. I had no doubt they could do it again. But in these times, they preferred to stay out of the politics of humanity and tend to their own issues.

I sat at the high table as a guest of honor. Diaz sat at Skully's right hand. Nala sat at Skye's left. Her place would have naturally been at the far end of the table. It wasn't sexist. I had a suspicion that the queens kept her close to keep her out of trouble. Her brothers kept slipping the little wildcat with pink-painted claws wary glances each time she reached for a dish.

Zane sat next to Nala and directly across from me. But I might as well have not even been in the room. He gave me not an ounce of his attention.

I'd showered after the hunt and changed into one of Skully's tanks. Mainly because I'd been sweaty, dirty, and there'd been blood under my nails. But I also wanted to get some of Tres's frankincense scent off of me for Zane's comfort. I had no idea whether or not my scent offended him any longer. As I said, he kept his head turned away from me.

But when a bowl of pomegranates was passed down the table, Zane examined the contents of the bowl. There were only two of the fruits left. Zane picked up the larger fruit, then he sat it back in the bowl. Instead, he picked up the smaller fruit that had a slight blemish on it. He put the less than perfect fruit on his plate and then pushed the bowl with the larger, unmarred specimen toward me. All without actually acknowledging me. But he didn't need to make eye contact. He knew my love of the fruit and he'd saved the best piece for me.

It was an absentminded action on his part, I know. But it gave me hope that maybe we could put all the secrets and hurt behind us one day and be friends again. Because, contrary to what I may have agreed to in my pact with Loren, Zane was my best friend.

After five hundred years together, he knew me better than anybody. He'd once said he knew me better than I knew myself. I knew it was true and I didn't want to lose that. I didn't want to lose another friend.

As Skye, Skully, and Diaz were friends to us both, and Nala was an incessant chatterbox, there wasn't much of a lull in the conversation at the head of the table. What appeared to be the pattern was that our friends would talk about a subject and I'd chime in while Zane would sit quietly or turn to Nala. Then at the start of a new subject, I'd go mute and Zane would speak to the group. But only for a few minutes until Nala would turn the conversation and his attention back around to her.

It was an orderly dance. A mature and harmonious promenade. The record scratch in the tune came from Nala.

"Omigosh." She fluttered her hands at her chest. "You should totally see the sketch Zaney made of me."

I actually gagged on my roast deer. Zaney? It made him sound like some cartoon character.

Zane had a similar reaction. His nose crinkled at his newly bestowed nickname. But he covered it with a swipe of his dinner napkin over his mouth.

"Like, I've had some of the greats draw me, like Banksy."

There was another gagging sound. But it wasn't me this time. I barely hid my smile as Zane tried to cover his distaste of the modern artist with a cough. Though he respected artists who used their skills for political and social commentary, he considered graffiti defamation.

Nala pulled the sketch from a handbag and unrolled it, holding it up for all to see. "The way Zaney captured my nipples is so surreal. They, like, look real."

The male Balam further down the table groaned. It was clear they didn't want to hear about their little sister's nipples.

"Can you imagine growing up with all these brothers?" Nala looked between me and Diaz, then back at me. "I guess you can." Then she frowned when she looked between me and Zane.

"We're not—" I said.

"We're not—" echoed Zane.

Diaz laughed.

"I mean it's cool," said Nala. "Like, that incest stuff went down in the olden times, right? What are you, like, two thousand or something?" She squinted at me. "Three thousand?"

"I'm the same age as him," I said.

Nala turned to admire Zane. "Isn't it so unfair that men can age so well and women just..." She sighed again as she turned back to me.

Zane wasn't even trying to hide his chuckle now. He sliced into his meat and placed a bit on his tongue.

"How's the boiled rabbit?" I asked. "I caught it myself."

He paused in his chewing. I could see the wheels in his brain turning as he recalled his remark earlier when he suggested that I had a fatal attraction to him. His eyes cut to mine for the first time that evening. He quirked a brow and began to chew again, more slowly this time.

"Thank you for asking, Nia," he said after he swallowed the piece of bunny.

I winced as he used my name.

"It's quite satisfying... Nia."

"Okay," I snapped. That was it. I was done. The thing about people who knew you well, they knew how to get under your skin without much effort. "Call me Nia one more time and see what happens."

The whole room went quiet. The air filled with anticipation as the Balam smelled a fight brewing in their midst. But their brows also furrowed as they couldn't determine exactly what this was all about.

Skye and Skully grinned their encouragement. To them, a good fight meant you cared. It made you stronger. And then, after a good fight, there was always the make-up part. But I wasn't interested in making up any longer. I just wanted him to stop it, stop treating me like I was some random acquaintance that meant nothing to him.

I looked to Skully for support. "He's doing it on purpose," I insisted.

Skully turned to Zane, who'd pulled on a mask of faux innocence.

"I thought that was her name?" said Nala.

"What would you prefer to be called?" Zane asked, his quiet voice patronizing. "Dr. Rivers?"

I winced.

"Beleheb?"

I grimaced.

My phone chose that moment to ring. The ringtone was "Arabian Nights" from the Disney movie *Aladdin*. I'd thought it was funny at the time I selected it. No one in the room laughed.

"You should probably get that..." said Zane. And then he added on after a pause, "Theta."

"You know what?" I scooted my chair back from the table. "I think I will."

"I really don't care." Zane shoved the rest of the rabbit off to the side of his plate.

"I didn't ask if you did." I stormed out of the room and out into the backyard, managing not to stick my tongue out at Zane on my retreat. "Hello."

It was in the five-second silence that followed that I realized my greeting was harsh. I loosened my grip on the phone, took a deep breath, and tried again.

"I'm sorry," I said. "Zane's here. He's being a complete asshole. He's not taking this breakup well."

There was another five seconds of silence and I wondered if the allergy was interfering with the phone connection. But then I heard Tres's voice clearly on the other end.

"I can fly out in an hour," said Tres. "I'll be there before midnight."

"No. Don't do that. I'm leaving in the morning. The queens, Diaz, and I are headed down to Chichén in the morning."

"*He's* not coming with you."

"*He* doesn't want to be around me any more than I want to be around him." I peered back into the house to see him leaning in to listen to Nala. "Besides, he's seeing someone else."

"Really?"

The amount of surprise in Tres's voice reminded me of the surprise on Diaz's face when I'd told him that Zane had broken up with me. I wondered if they both knew about the whole Zane-had-only-been-with-me thing. But I did not want to talk about my ex-lover's sex life with my new lover. Even though Tres and I weren't exactly lovers yet. Instead of bringing up Zane, I looked for another wedge to place between Tres and me.

"Tres, did you try and buy land here in Holmul?"

I could hear him thinking. "Is this going to lead to an argument?"

"No. I don't think so. A monument there was damaged—"

"And you think I did it?"

"No. I don't."

"But Skye and Skully do?"

I sighed.

"I'm sorry," he said. "It makes me uncomfortable that the woman I'm trying to get closer to is in a den of wolves who all have it out for me."

"Balam are not canine. They're feline."

"I know," he said. "But a den of cats doesn't sound sinister at all."

I chuckled. "No, it doesn't. Not everyone here is against you. Diaz is always on your side."

"Really? Skully gave him back his testicles long enough to make a decision on his own?"

I tried not to laugh, but that was kind of funny.

"Why Chichén?" Tres asked.

"Chichén Itzá is where the serpent shadow climbs the pyramid."

"But it's not either of the solstices," said Tres.

"No, but I'm hoping to gather more information by looking at the stelas inside the observatory. Hopefully I'll have some answers tomorrow."

CHAPTER SIXTEEN

Immortals could go without sleep for long periods and still function. I'd once stayed awake for two weeks straight after a dig in the Arctic went south. The entire human crew had been lost to the elements, but I'd survived and kept moving. I knew that if I stopped, I would succumb to the elements too. So I walked in the snow for twelve days before I found civilization again. I'd started hallucinating at the end of the first week.

I would see paintings in the sky and sculptures in the snow. I swore that Zane was with me, talking to me, demanding I took the next step and then the next that would lead me back into the warmth of his arms. This was back at the earlier part of the century, so phone lines were crude, but I was able to get a message to him. I have no idea how, but he arrived within two days for a journey that should've taken him a week.

He'd wrapped me up in his arms. All the chill and frostbite had melted away. I slept for days against his chest as I healed.

I slept peacefully after I got off the phone with Tres. It was a dreamless sleep of nothingness. My mind was so tired that it couldn't even picture darkness. There were no visions of a black chasm in the earth swallowing anyone whole. Perhaps that was because I knew that Zane was down the hall, safe. Even if he might be in the clutches of a hellcat.

Whatever. He could do with his life what he wanted. Just so long as he lived. The bastard.

Even though I was surrounded by two of my kind, I woke in the morning feeling strong and refreshed. I slipped into a pair of cargo pants loaned to me by Skully and a floral top loaned to me by Skye. I hadn't brought any clothes with me to or from my island, but I had brought some of the tools I'd need.

I filled the various pockets with things I'd need on today's outing. I slipped a handheld resistivity meter in one pocket. The meter could measure the flow of electricity through the ground as well as determine the differences in soil composition. Archaeologists used it to survey for underground structures.

I also had more common tools such as a trowel to dig, a sieve to sift through the dirt, and a brush to clean off the surface of my findings so that I could determine their importance if any.

I gathered my things, strapping a couple of daggers to my thighs. I didn't think I'd need the weapons. Chichén Itzá was a tourist spot. I just felt naked without a blade somewhere on my body.

I headed down to the dining area for breakfast. The Balam didn't store anything. Everything was consumed after it was caught. Anything leftover was consumed when they woke the next day before they went on the next hunt.

There were a few strips of rabbit left over. I popped a couple of pieces in my mouth while I waited for the others to come down. Slowly, the shifters made their way down the stairs. Some headed outside for a run in their natural skin. Others headed into the den and fired up a gaming console. A few others headed into the biggest man cave I'd ever seen and turned on four large-screen television sets that displayed a different soccer game on each.

Finally, the queens and Diaz made their appearance. We all headed out to one of the trucks and strapped in for our road trip to Mexico.

Zane hadn't come downstairs when we pulled out. Neither had Nala. I refused to think about the implications of that.

He clearly didn't like her. He was polite to her while she threw herself at him. There was no desire in his eyes when he looked at her. Trust me, I knew. I'd seen his hooded eyes wide with desire more times than I could count.

I'd seen the sketch he'd drawn of her. There wasn't that much detail in her nipples. He'd spent more time on the drawing depicting the coat of her jaguar skin than he had on the one featuring the curves of her womanhood.

But it wasn't any of my business if he wanted to use her to try and make me jealous. Because clearly, that's what he was doing. Everyone could see it. They all were just too polite to say anything.

Diaz was at the wheel while Skully had her hand in his lap. Her hand was more in his crotch, but whatever. The drive from Guatemala to Mexico was ten hours, and he drove the whole way with only one stop to relieve himself that took about thirty minutes with both he and Skully occupying the bathroom.

Skye sat next to me in the back. Well, she lay next to me and catnapped the entire way. I supposed she was as exhausted as I was about the whole Zane and Nala thing, not that it was a thing. Skye shifted in the back seat, searching for more comfort. Or maybe having a nightmare about a screeching cat running her claws down Zane's back, or whatever. Skye let out a sigh and settled. Well, at least her nightmare was over for the time being.

I turned my attention back to the matter at hand as I tried to puzzle out how I'd gain entrance to the underworld of Xibalba through one of the monuments erected for the Mayan gods.

There were hundreds of limestone pyramids, temples, and palaces throughout the Mayan empire. Not all of them were still intact. The Europeans who came to this new world had devastated this land and much of its historical record.

Thousands of Mayan writings and books were burned by conquistadors and Christians who thought the works to be of the devil. Even today, these places so rich with human history weren't a priority to archaeologists. Though much had been destroyed, there was so much to learn if they simply turned over the dirt.

They had turned over the dirt of two structures at Chichén Itzá. They were El Castillo, the castle, and El Caracol, the observatory.

At various times of the year, the windows of El Caracol, which literally translated to "spiral-shaped" or "the snail," captured astronomical events that were easily observable from its high platform. With its winding staircase and dome cap, it was easy to see the changes in the sky over the flatlands of the Yucatan with the naked eye. In one window it was clear to see the arrival of Venus as it appeared on the horizon in the west and disappeared again in the eastern horizon every 584 days. The Mayans noted that five of these cycles equaled eight solar years.

But the observatory showed off more than the movements of the second planet. It was possible to see twenty-nine astronomical events from the tower including eclipses, equinoxes, and solstices. Well, it had been possible. Since one portion of the tower had been lost, an observer could only view twenty events now.

I was more interested in the castle. Like many Mayan temples, El Castillo had three hundred and sixty-five steps. Ninety-one on each side of the structure plus the temple platform. Add that all up and you get the same amount for the number of days in the year. Twice a year during the fall and spring equinoxes, when the sun crossed the line in the sky above the equator, the planet and the celestial body aligned in such a way that the shadow of a snake appeared to slither down the steps of the castle.

It was a visual marvel. I was a bit surprised that when the religious conquerors from Spain first saw it, they didn't think the climbing snake was a work of the devil and include the castle in their campaign of destruction. But El Castillo had survived.

Another name for the castle was the Temple of Kukulcan. Kukulcan was the name of the serpent deity. There were sculptures of the serpent on the side of the northern balustrade. Large heads that looked more like dragons than snakes with their mouths open and their tongues protruding.

We passed by rows of great pillars that had once been a marketplace. I had vague memories of weaving through this place and marveling at the trinkets available. I also remembered feeling sick to my stomach as I'd looked up on the walls that surrounded the area to see a line of human skulls.

The skulls were placed there as an intimidation

factor. They belonged to the enemies of the king. But sacrifice was a thing of honor in this ancient culture.

Beyond the pillars and the walls was what might be called a basketball court. It was a wide-open field. On a high wall was a hoop where players would shoot a ball. Here's the kicker: the winner of the game won the honor of being sacrificed. Needless to say, I didn't spend too much time in Chichén Itzá during that point in history.

It wasn't the time of year of the solstice, but there were still tons of tourists milling around. Their camera flashes lit up the scenery as the sun began to set. Many of their faces showed disappointment when the shadows stayed on the ground instead of crawling down the steps of the monument.

My eyes perked up when a bronzed god strode forward from the midst of the crowd. Striding forward through the daypack wearers and the locals who were hawking overpriced bottled water was an unmistakable figure. His grin was as wide as the snake statues once he reached me.

"What are you doing here?" I asked Tres.

He was out of his normal business suit and in khaki slacks and a cotton shirt. He slipped his sunshades from his nose to the crown of his head and his dark eyes blazed down at me in the setting sun.

"I thought you might be able to use my expertise," he said, nodding at the ancient structure.

I looked from him to the castle and back again. "You built El Castillo?"

Before he could answer, Skye did it for him. "No. He didn't. He never built any temples or pyramids in Central or South America."

"But he has built eyesores that scrape the sky and cut through our lands," said Skully.

Skully glared at her mate, who'd given her a pinch in her side. Probably meant to quiet her. Instead, she growled. Diaz ignored his beloved and walked forward with his arms open for Tres.

"It's good to see you, *manito*."

Tres came into Diaz's open embrace with a grin of his own and a loud clap on the back. Then he straightened and turned to the queens. He bowed his head in deference. But the two eyed him skeptically. It was about to be a long night.

CHAPTER SEVENTEEN

We waited until sunset before we made our approach. The tourists had all packed up their cameras and gone back to their hotels. The locals had stored away their waters and trinkets and returned to their homes. With the coast clear, it was pretty easy to gain access to the structure. Getting inside was a different matter. Luckily, we had an accomplished engineer in our midst.

Tres reached into his pocket, pulled out his wallet, and handed the night guard a very large bill. Then, magically, the bolted door that led to the interior of the structure opened for us. An engineer using his best weapon: capitalism.

Skye and Skully sniffed and rolled their eyes.

They had likely been looking forward to knocking some heads together to gain access. Diaz chuckled as he took the point—that is, after he shouldered his way past Skully. She didn't take kindly to being treated daintily.

I brought up the rear with Tres as the door shut behind us. I handed Tres and Diaz headlamps. Skye and Skully could see in the dark with their supernatural eyes.

We made our way down a narrow interior staircase. Diaz had to turn sideways after his broad shoulders got stuck twice in the passageway.

Aside from coming here in the ancient past, I'd also been back in the more recent past. I'd traveled here during an excavation back in the 1930s. Back then the jungle had begun to reclaim these structures as the people had turned their backs on the old ways.

I'd been to this part of the pyramid before. We were currently in what was known as the Hall of Offerings. When the excavation team had come here in the twentieth century, they'd found some remnant offerings inside. There was a box of objects encrusted with coral, obsidian, and turquoise. Fantastic finds, but pretty mundane in comparison to what we found in the next room.

Our small band of Balam and Immortals stepped into the hall that had been dubbed the Chamber of Sacrifice. On the back wall of the stone room were human bones set into the wall. A statue of a red jaguar made of jade faced the north-northeastern corner.

The jaguar statue had led some to believe that this interior was built on top of another structure. But they'd never found it. And like much of Central America, the western scientists lost interest, packed up, and hadn't been back since. The furthest they'd gotten inside was to this chamber with the jaguar throne and its head facing at an odd angle.

Tres ran his hand over the walls. I knew from past experience that he was looking for a lever in the wall that might lead us to a hidden entry.

I pulled out my resistivity meter and flipped it on. We didn't have tools like these back in the early twentieth century. We had to roll up our sleeves and dig if we wanted to see what was beneath the surface, if anything. The dial immediately jumped off the scale, indicating that there was something below the ground.

"There's water down there," I said.

"Yes," said Skye. "We know."

I let the device drop to my side and faced the twins. "What do you mean you know?"

"This whole structure was built on a cenote," said Skully.

A cenote was a sinkhole. It was formed by limestone and acted as an incubator, keeping the interior humid, much like a wine cellar or my underground cave.

"The priests would sacrifice adolescent girls by tossing them into the sinkhole as fertile offerings to the gods," said Skye.

They both turned up their hands at my gasp.

"It was before our time," said Skully.

But she didn't sound wholly sympathetic. Like I said, violence and sacrifice were a way of life. The Mayans believed that sacrifice to the gods was an honor and a privilege, one they fought for.

I turned my attention back to the meter and its findings. There wasn't just water down there. My readings were telling me that there was another structure. I paced the ground, mentally calculating the area.

"I think there's another pyramid down here," I said, then turned to Tres. "There has to be a way down. Have you found anything?"

Tres was standing in front of a stela on the wall.

There was a line of stone slabs. I walked over to him and, adding my light to his, focused on the symbols. How had I not seen these before? Or maybe I had and didn't give them enough attention because they made no sense.

Meanings swam in my head, turning over and in and out like a kaleidoscope. I saw the word for door, another for snake, and another for the planet Venus.

"It looks like this would be the opening," said Tres. He pointed to the stela on the wall with the symbol of Venus. "What if the interior was built from the inside out? Meaning a door with no handle. You have to push your way out from the other side; you can't pull."

"But if the God Twins came out this door, how would they get back in?" I said.

My attention turned back to the statue of the jaguar with the head facing at an odd angle. I looked in the direction that the head faced. When the sun set on the equinoxes of this building, the serpent's head rested at the top. When the sun set on the serpent-shaped mounds of La Sufricaya or the more widely known serpent mound in Ohio, the disk rested on the heads of those monuments. But even if the sun did set, it wouldn't reach this statue.

Tres looked from the jaguar statue to the stela.

"The light wouldn't hit it from this angle. It may have been moved."

"Where does it need to be?" asked Skully, momentarily forgetting her dislike of the man.

Tres twisted his lip. I knew he was making the calculations in his head. "Here."

He reached down and braced himself to push the statue. But my yelp stopped him.

"This is hundreds of years old," I said, my voice high-pitched as everyone stared mutely at me. "I'm just saying be careful."

Tres and Diaz moved the statue slowly, inch by inch, from the corner of the room where it had been shoved. As it approached the place where Tres had indicated, we all heard an audible click.

Everyone froze and held their breath. Tres and Diaz stepped back from the statue. We all waited with bated breath. I'm not sure if we thought a door would open and allow us passage. Or if the twins would beckon us inside for a game of ball.

Nothing happened. The moonlight shone in through a sliver of light from somewhere above. The sliver landed on the body of the jaguar but nowhere else. No opening illuminated. No panel creaked open.

"I don't think it's the right time," Tres said. "You

said that's a depiction of Venus? Maybe it's on a Venetian calendar and not the solstice."

"When's the next arrival of Venus on the horizon?" asked Diaz.

"About five hundred days from now," said Skye.

That was over a year from now. I didn't think I could afford that much time. Someone I loved could die before the stars aligned, and there was nothing I could do. I couldn't reach up and rearrange the heavens. I couldn't dig my way around the wall that would lead me to another land. I couldn't even bust down the emotional wall that Zane had put between us.

My frustration zeroed in on the jaded jaguar. I shoved at the statue. Then I kicked the priceless piece of art. A crack rent the leg of the stone beast.

I couldn't even feel upset at the damage I'd done. I needed to get down there. It was life or death. But even with my strength and my cunning, the doors to the underworld wouldn't open.

sat on the thousand-count sheets of the luxury hotel room in a fluffy terrycloth robe that weighed more than I did. The dust and grime had been washed from my body in the opulent shower that housed an assortment of indulgent soaps and shampoos and perfumes. I was squeaky clean and floral-scented, but I still felt grimy and battered.

The bruise I had from pounding the jaguar statue was still visible along my pinky finger down to my wrist. My heel throbbed and the pain radiated dully up my calf from kicking at the statue. I'd only made a hairline crack in the ancient object, but my old bones were rattled. No wonder, since I'd been around my kind for two weeks straight now and the allergies were in full effect. My healing and reflexes were slowed. My body was weary and my spirit low.

I was trying to focus on the bright side through the pain in my limbs and head. That bright side was that I had been right. There were doors to the underworld. The problem was that they were on a celestial clock and would only open from the inside.

I wasn't about to give up. I just needed a moment to rest. Staring at the plush pillow, I willed myself to fall into its softness and sink into sleep. But my body stayed upright, refusing to take even a moment's repose while danger was still brewing somewhere beneath the surface, ready to snatch away someone I cared about.

Plus, I didn't want to face my worst fears in my dreams. I hadn't dreamed last night, and I'm pretty sure that was because I knew that Zane was within arm's reach. In another woman's arms, true, but safe. But I couldn't see him now, and the anxiety in my heart was rising.

I thumbed the screen of my phone. The profile picture of him on my device was one of him sitting at his easel. A small smile played at his lips; paint was also just below his lower lip. While he'd been painting me, I'd been snapping photos of him. I had a whole roll on my phone, but I didn't scroll through them now. I also didn't tap the text or talk button on my phone to reach out to him. I'd already been rejected by a jaded jaguar back inside the temple; I didn't need the treatment again from a flesh-and-blood man who wouldn't open up to me either.

I rose from the bed and headed out to the balcony. Though we were in a city, the stars shone bright across the night sky. I could make out a number of the constellations.

I hadn't had any interest in the stars until Zane began painting them. All my attention had been focused on the ground and the wonders in the dirt. But he'd taught me to look up. He'd pondered about someday going to the stars and writing my name in stardust.

It had been romantic at the time, when I was stupid in love with him. It had been a way to keep connected when there were countries and deserts and oceans between us. Now, with only a manageable number of miles between us, we'd never been so distant.

I spotted the Andromeda galaxy shining bright in the heavens. It was the most distant of the star arrangements that could be seen with the naked eye. Being that my eyes weren't entirely human, I saw the elliptical-shaped galaxy clearly.

Greek myths told the story of the young Andromeda, who'd been chained and left for the sea monster as a sacrifice to the gods to save the rest of her people. The story had some basis in truth, though Andromeda wasn't Greek. She was an Ethiopian princess. She'd been offered up to Poseidon, the very real Olympian. But she'd been in love with another from her homeland, Perseus. Perseus wasn't the mythical slayer of Medusa nor the owner of famed winged slippers. But he had come in and scooped her out of Greece and run off with her.

I don't know what truly happened to them after that, except that they were immortalized in the stars. What I did know was that story was yet another example of myths, legends, and prophecies not being recorded or foretold verbatim. Andromeda hadn't been sacrificed. She'd gotten married.

Igraine's prophecy was likely only an interpretation. It didn't mean that someone would actually, physically die. Maybe it would be a spiritual death, like heartbreak or a rebirth.

The thought didn't settle the anxiety riding a roller coaster between my head, through my heart, and down to my gut. I looked away from the stars and palmed my phone again. My fingers itched to hit the talk button. But I knew I would get no response from him. Or worse, he'd dole out pure disdain across the line. And I'd promised him space.

Well, I'd promised that I wouldn't call him directly. I could hear Diaz and Skully going at it in the next room even though the walls were thick. I'm sure the hotel guests from the bottom floor on up could hear those two animals.

On the other side of my room, Skye had picked up a couple of silver foxes and was giving them the ride of their lives. Skye didn't give a man a second glance unless he had a bit of salt and pepper in his hair. I was a little worried about the gentlemen and their hearts being able to keep pace with her. They thought they were toying with a coed, but little did they know they'd stepped into the lair of a centuries-old cougar.

I didn't have the patience to wait either of them out. Looking back down at my phone, I tapped out a different number. The phone rang a number of times before someone picked up. The voice on the other end came on scratchy.

"Oy, Nia."

"Hey, Delta. Hi. How are you? Where are you?"

"I'm about to head up Annapurna on a solo climb."

The Annapurna Massif in the Himalayas was

one of the hardest mountains to climb in the world. Over fifty people attempting to summit had died; less than two hundred have succeeded.

I should've chastised Delta. She knew our lives were potentially in danger and she was doing something that could break her neck. But she'd always been this way. When you lived as long as we did and you were impervious to most things, you looked for something to make you feel alive.

Interestingly enough, the anxiety that had settled like a rock in my gut didn't rise as I heard her clapping her hands together, likely chalking up for her climb. I didn't feel that bone-deep dread, though she was putting herself directly in the path of peril. I only got that feeling for Zane.

The knot in my gut twisted. I would not let that happen, no matter how much he hated me, no matter what an ass he became to me. I could lower my pride for a few minutes if it meant he'd live another day.

"So, Delta, you talk to Zane today?"

"Uh, no. Isn't he with you? You're all in Guatemala with those luscious queens."

Delta purred into the phone, making a good imitation of the sounds of the Balam queens in their jaguar form. Delta had given up on men a few centuries ago and only dated women. She was old enough for Skye to take an interest, but unfortunately for Delta, Skye had had a good relationship with her mother. The Mayan queen only had daddy issues.

"I'm actually in Mexico with Tresor," I said.

"Really? Is that soap opera of you three still going on? I thought you'd gotten over that back in Uruk, or was it Greece? I can't keep track of the saga you have with those two. It's dizzying the way..."

The phone crackled for a second and her voice went muffled. But it only lasted a couple of seconds before she came back clearly.

"But no. I haven't spoken to him since he touched down in Guatemala a couple of weeks ago."

A couple of weeks? He'd only been with the queens for the last week. What else had he been doing in Guatemala?

"The Balam park isn't far from Mexico," Delta was saying. "Why don't you hop over and see him for yourself?"

"He doesn't want to talk to me."

"You two had another row?" Delta sighed. "Listen, sweets, he may say that he doesn't want to talk to you, but you know it's not true. He's been tightly and happily wrapped around your finger since the beginning of time."

Maybe. But all that was unraveling now. I was terrified that we wouldn't make amends before our time was up.

"Listen," I said, "if you talk to him, don't tell him I called."

"What's this about, Nia? Is it the witch's prophecy? You know I don't believe in that hoo-hah. Epsilon and Vau's deaths were a fluke, and I have no love lost for Yod. He got what was coming to him with all the death and destruction he dealt for centuries."

That warmed me that she didn't blame me for Yod's death. But it did not loosen the knot in my gut that something bad was going to happen.

"I won't spy on Zane for you," Delta continued. "But I'll let you know his general state of health if it'll help you sleep at night."

"It would help me sleep. Thank you, Delta. Go on and get back to your mountain. But please use harnesses, for me."

I got off the phone with Delta. It made me feel better that I could reach out to her in the future. But it did nothing for how I felt now.

I knew Zane wasn't in any immediate danger. He

was at a compound filled with shifters. The worst thing that would happen to him was that Nala would mark him with her claws. Honestly, I'd prefer Nala have him than that abyss I saw in my dreams.

The bathroom door opened and Tres walked out in a towel and nothing else. I'd been so wrapped up in my own drama that I'd forgotten he was there. He came to stand in the middle of the room but didn't approach me. His gaze went from my eyes to my ear.

"Is that him?"

The phone was still at my ear even though I'd hung up with Delta. I pulled it from my face and looked down at it. Then I looked back up at him.

There was resignation on his face. I played his words back over in my head again. There wasn't exactly a question mark at the end of his statement. He expected me to run back to Zane. He'd said it's what I always did.

"No. I mean, yes. But not how you think." I set the phone aside and faced Tres directly. "I was talking to Delta. About Zane. Because he doesn't want to talk to or see me."

Tres came and sat down on the bed next to me. Even though he'd washed, he still smelled heavily of incense. It was buried in his skin. Though Zane had

had such an adverse reaction to it, I found that I didn't. It was a comfort.

"I keep having nightmares," I confessed. "That it's him. Zane. That he's the one who dies in the prophecy. I'm not trying to get back with him. But I don't want him to die. That's why I need to get to the Xibalba. I need to get there and stop this, whatever is about to happen, so that I know he's safe. And then I can tell him to go to hell and mean it."

I took a deep breath, and my shoulders shook with the effort. Tres brushed my loose hair off my shoulders and offered a small smile. There was understanding in his gaze where I thought there would be annoyance.

Here we were again. We both sat on a bed, nearly nude. Instead of ravaging each other, he listened while I went on about my ex.

"How can I help?" he asked.

I offered him the same small smile in return. I ran a hand down his bicep, trying to soak in his strength. His skin was still wet from the shower.

"Can you move heaven and earth?" I asked. "Particularly the path of Venus up?"

"For you, I would if I could." And then he frowned. He turned his gaze from me to the open window and the starry sky beyond. "You know,

Venus and the equinox aren't the only astronomical movements."

"I know. There are twenty-nine astronomical events that can be tracked from earth."

"What's the next one?"

I wasn't sure. "You think there could be another alignment happening at another monument sooner?"

I reached back for my discarded phone and pulled open a search engine. Why hadn't I thought of that instead of wallowing and whining to a girlfriend?

"There's a summer solstice happening over the northwest of America next week," I said.

"Do you know any monuments created by Native Americans in North America that interlink with celestial events?"

"There are tons."

"Any that have something in common with El Castillo?"

I thought for a moment, running through my Rolodex of protected lands and sites. My memories of dirt were always clear in my head. In addition to pyramids, and trails, and preserved villages, there were a number of mounds. One mound, in particular, came to mind.

"I think the common theme of the doorways is the symbol of the serpent." I tapped my phone to get a closer look. The solstice took place midsummer when the earth's axis inclined, or tilted, toward the sun. Right there on the screen, I saw the mound I had in mind. "I need to get to Ohio."

CHAPTER NINETEEN

"The summer solstice occurs next week," I began.

The queens nodded and hmm'd at my words, not giving me their full attention. Skye was busy watching the asses of men walking by. As always, she ignored the pert, high asses of the coeds on the streets of Mexico and instead glued her gaze to the silver-haired foxes who strolled by.

On the other end of the table, Skully nipped at Diaz's ear and chin. She's the one that hmm'd, but I don't think that was in acknowledgment of my statement about the eclipse. I was certain the next part would get their attention.

I looked to Tres at my side. He shrugged and

took a swig of his beer. Okay, I'd get straight to the point then.

"I need to get permission to dig up a Native American burial mound," I said.

That got a reaction. Skye's head whipped from the fox she'd been cornering with her gaze back to me. Skully tore her teeth away from Diaz's earlobe. He gasped in pain and pinched at his sensitive flesh. But the grin on his lips told me he wasn't the least bit put out about the sting.

"You want to desecrate our ancestral lands?" said Skye.

Though the queens were of Mayan descent, and though they'd fought bloody wars with various groups and tribes up north, they looked at all indigenous peoples of the Americas as their subjects.

Skully's eyes tore from me and went to Tres. "What's this about?"

Tres sighed and held up his hands, ready to begin a defense of a war he wasn't raging.

"It has nothing to do with his business," I said.

Skully raised a dubious eyebrow, which remained arched at Tres.

"I need to see if there's a doorway to Xibalba

beneath the Serpent Mound in Fort Ancient territory."

Skully slowly gave me back her attention.

There were many mounds built throughout America, mainly along the fertile valleys of the rivers of Mississippi, Illinois, Missouri, and Ohio. Many of the ancient mounds had been destroyed as the New World was colonized and farming spread across the region.

The Serpent Mound stood out chief amongst them. It was the largest serpent effigy known in the world. Shaped like a serpent with a large ovular head and a coiled tail, the mound of seven coils stretched one thousand and three hundred feet, rising up to three feet above the ground. It looked like a mossy sand castle sculpture. But it didn't wash away with the tide. The mound had weathered hundreds, maybe even thousands, of years of storms, wars, and modernization.

Twice a year something spectacular would happen. On the summer solstice, the head of the serpent aligned with the sunset. The coiled tail pointed to the sunrise of the winter solstice. The curves in the body of the snake aligned with the lunar phases and the equinoxes. If there was a stela down beneath the dirt of the mound, then this would be a frequent door that had convenient hours of business.

I hadn't visited the site in over a hundred years. Archaeologists continued to debate how it had been made, and by whom. I had vague memories of the site, but it had never held my attention as I wasn't allowed to dig around it.

"It's not entirely up to us," said Skye. "If you want to disturb ancestral land you'll need to get the chiefs' permission."

"That's why I need your help," I said. "I don't know these new Mohegan chiefs."

Both Skully and Skye sighed. In tandem, they leaned back in their chairs and crossed their arms over their chests. The only way I could tell them apart in this moment, aside from Skye's pastel top and Skully's dark tank, was because Diaz had an arm draped over Skully's shoulder.

"We do need to pay them a visit," said Skye.

"They were meant to pay us a visit after they claimed domination," said Skully.

"It was a power play that they didn't. And then they sent us that spoiled loner princess to raise."

"We need to go up there and challenge them."

"Too right. Those cocky bastards are due for a bruising."

"We can't let disrespect like this stand."

"Guys," I said. My head was spinning as the two spoke over each other, making it unclear which woman was speaking at any moment. "Can we—I mean, can you two—challenge them after I get permission to dig? If it's not too much trouble?"

"I know them," said Tres. "I built one of their casinos. And they prefer to be called chairmen, not chiefs."

Another eye roll from Skully, followed by a grunt from Skye.

"Another reason I don't like them," said Skully. "They don't live according to the old ways."

"They don't hunt for their food."

"They have private chefs."

"And restaurants."

"They make a profit."

"Who does that?"

After speaking in harmonic tandem once more, both queens ended their tirade by turning to glare at Tres.

"This is a life or death situation," I said, looking between the three. "I'd really appreciate someone's help."

"I'll make a call." Tres got up from the table, palming his cell phone.

"I'll give you a hand," said Diaz.

The men walked away, leaving the three of us alone. We sat at an outside bar. There were three empty pitchers in front of the queens. My full glass was barely touched. Shifters had even faster metabolisms than Immortals. Skye signaled the waiter for another round.

"I really don't know what you see in him, Bele," said Skully.

"He's so young," said Skye.

"He's older than you," I said.

Skye sniffed and refilled her glass.

I knew both of them were Team Zane. But they were just going to have to get used to the fact that we were apart now. Of course, I was one to talk, I know. My own phone burned in my pocket and my fingers itched to text Zane.

The bad feeling in my stomach had not dissipated, even with this new, workable plan forming. Regardless of whether or not the Mohegan gave me their permission, I was going to Ohio. I'd find a way beneath the Serpent Mound and hopefully find an entry into the underworld.

But I'd still have to wait a few more days. The solstice wouldn't happen until the end of the week. I wondered if I could convince Zane to come with me to Ohio, just so I could keep an eye on him. But that would be seriously awkward while we both pursued other relationships.

Needing to shut my brain off, I turned away from my friends and my problems to look at the dancing. A father dressed in jeans spun a little girl swathed in crinoline up in his arms. The child giggled as her chubby hands clung to her father's neck. From the corner of my eye, I saw the twins watching the display too.

"Do you think our lives would have been different if we'd had our fathers in it?" I asked.

"Different how?" asked Skye.

"I don't know?" I shrugged. "Maybe we'd be normal, capable of having a normal relationship. No fear of commitment."

"I'm in a committed relationship," said Skully as she caught sight of Diaz making his way back to us in the crowd.

"I'm not afraid of commitment," said Skye. "I'm just not interested in having it with a man, especially a human one. I'm committed to my family, to the cubs that get brought into this world by irresponsible gods and then left to fend for themselves. There are a lot of animals that leave their young to their own defenses. It's sink or swim, fly or fall, eat or get eaten. That's natural."

The father and daughter duo danced with the girl stepping on her father's feet. It was a scene straight out of a Hallmark card. As the two laughed, an adult-sized version of the child came into the mix. The father leaned down and kissed the mother and then brought the woman into the fold so that they sandwiched the child between them. The little girl was surrounded by love.

I heard a sniff beside me. When I turned, Skully was looking up at the moon with glistening eyes. Skye was looking down at her phone.

"I'd better check in at the park," said Skye. "No telling what the cubs have gotten into."

"They're unsupervised," said Diaz as he and Tres rejoined the table. "Which means they've likely invited a bunch of female day-trippers onto the property and they're all rutting against some tree."

"The chairmen said to come up anytime," said Tres as he sat next to me. "They reserved us the penthouse for a week."

I told the anxiety that rose in my chest that that would be nice. I could go and explore my new relationship with Tres while Zane was safe at the park. True, in the clutches of Nala, but at least he'd be safe. That was what was most important. I could go to the mound and see if I could get through a door, and after I came out the other end I could finally get on with my life, properly.

I turned back to Skye as she rejoined the table. "Everything okay at the park?"

"They're partying," she said, "of course."

"Zane's responsible," I said. "He won't let anything get too far out of hand."

"Zane's not there. He left shortly after we did."

CHAPTER TWENTY

There had been a time when I dreamed of masked men strapping me down to an altar, skinning me alive, and then drinking my bones. There had been a time where I'd dreamed of ancient temple builders having their souls stripped from them in mass ritual sacrifice. In comparison to the nightmares I'd been having the past week, including the one I couldn't wake from now, those dreams of the past would have been a welcome reprieve.

Behind my eyelids, the darkness consumed me. I knew I was dreaming, but I felt the shadows cloying at me. The shade settled around my shoulders like a shawl, the murkiness hung like a fringe swishing at my back and sides as I tried to find my way through. And then I felt him.

He stood near me, next to me, but so far away from me. It was almost as though I wasn't dreaming. This was how Zane and I were in real life these days. Physically close, but emotionally on opposite sides of the planet.

But then, for just one second, he reached out and brought me to him. His chest pressed against mine. He put his hand on my hip with his thumb rubbing just below my belly button and his fingertips touching my sacrum. When I looked up at him, his face was illuminated in a strange blue light. But he was so distant. Though he held me close, his dark-roast eyes, which had once been so open and vibrant, were closed to me.

His grip loosened and then fell away completely. He took a step back from me, and then another. I reached for him, but I couldn't move. I couldn't go after him as the distance increased between us.

Once he was just beyond my reach, he raised his hand out toward me. Our fingertips met. I knew he was readying to take the last step, the one where the darkness would swallow him. But he hesitated. It looked like he would stop, like he would make his way back to me. Instead, his gaze flicked over my shoulder.

Following Zane's trajectory, I turned to see Tres standing right behind me. Tres reached out and wrapped his hand around my middle. He pulled me into the cocoon of his warm chest. When I turned back around, Zane was gone.

I woke with my former lover's name on my lips. It tore from my chest and filled the inner cabin of the plane. When I opened my eyes, Tres was bent over my seat.

One of his hands cradled mine. The other was gently shaking my shoulder. Like Zane's face had been in the dream, Tres's face was a stiff, expressionless mask as he gazed down at me. Of course it was. I had jerked out of his grasp and called out another man's name.

At the other side of the cabin, Skully raised her brow at me with a look that said *I told you so*. Diaz had his arm draped around her while he cringed, his lips making the shape of the word *ouch*. I shut my eyes, wishing I could sink back into the nightmare. But there was no hiding. I opened my eyes and turned back to Tres.

His dark eyes, which had been so open only days ago, were shuttered. He looked down; only a sliver of the whites of his eyes were visible to me. I reached for his hand and cradled it to me. He let me, not moving from his protective crouch.

"I'm sorry," I said. "I know I'm being unfair to you right now. You're flying me around the world so I can make sure my ex-boyfriend doesn't die because of a witch's prophecy and a couple of bad dreams."

"The apology is nice," said Tres. "The acknowledgment that I'm enlarging my eco-footprint on account of your whims is even better."

That got me a raised brow, and I could see into his gaze once more. He searched my eyes. I don't think he found what he was looking for because he sighed and looked down at our interlocked fingers.

"Zane's a grown man, Nia. And he's not stupid. He has a broken heart right now. The worst he'll do is go graffiti a perfectly good wall or make an eyesore of a sculpture made of recycled material or write emo poetry."

"He's never written poetry."

"Oh, yes, he did." Tres snorted. "Remember, he was my friend before he was your boyfriend. I had to listen to that crap."

Great. Just another thing I didn't know about the men in my life. Now that I knew more about Tres and Zane's past, Tres seemed more willing to open up about Zane. I got the feeling by the way he rolled his eyes just now that he might have missed Zane over the past few centuries the way I was missing him over the past few weeks.

I had suspected that there was some interrupted bromance between the two when we all were in the Gongyi province of China facing off against the Lin Kuei. Tres, Loren, and I had been trapped in—get this—a cave. I really had to reassess my work underground. While we were bound inside the earth, Zane had come to our rescue. My rescue, actually.

In the heat of the battle, Zane had held a blade to Tres. It looked as though, for a moment, he'd thought of slitting Tres's throat. Instead, Zane wound up cutting Tres's bindings. At that time, neither man had mentioned their past brotherhood to me.

In our past relationship, Zane had only listened passively as I'd complained about Tres and his business dealings. Until recently, Tres had only grumbled about my tendency to go back to Zane. He hadn't mentioned their past until my island.

"He may not be at the top of my Christmas list," Tres was saying now, "and I may have tried to wring his neck a few times in the past, but I don't want to see him... you know."

"Yeah," I said. "I know."

"Excuse me, Mr. Mohandis?" The model stewardess came before us. "The captain requests a word."

Tres rose from his seat and headed to the front of the plane. Once he was out of sight, I headed over to Skully and Diaz. It was just in time too.

"Can you believe he has a bedroom and shower in there?" said Skully. "Hey, baby, let's go try out the mattress. I wanna mark some territory."

"Diaz?" I called before my friend stuck her claws in him and I lost his attention for the rest of the flight.

Diaz turned to me, his gaze foggy as he watched Skully's hips sashay through Tres's bedroom door.

"Any word?" I asked once he managed to focus on me.

Diaz blinked, clearly trying to grasp the meaning of the two monosyllabic words I'd uttered to him. I could tell when the details of our previous conversation made it through his passion-muddled brain.

He shook his head in the negative.

"Can you try again?" I asked.

"I've texted him, and I've called him. Both messages went undelivered. He probably turned his phone off. He's fine, *manita*. He just needs time to heal. You two have been through this before. You separate and then you find your way back to each other. Regardless of who might be between you. You and Zane are like magnets. Like me and my queen."

"Diaz," sing-songed Skully. "I'm going to count to *diez*…"

Diaz gave me a shrug, and his attention, as well as his whole person, was gone before Skully got to *uno*.

I headed back to my seat and accepted a coffee from the flight attendant. I didn't want to fall back into the grips of sleep. The caffeine wasn't necessary. Diaz and Skully kept the whole plane awake with their amorous activities. Only Skye slept through the raucous noise. Tres stayed in the office area until the plane landed.

Shortly after the wheels hit the tarmac we were met with a stretch limo. Skye turned up her nose, but she dove into the limo and then squished her bum around on the seat. Skully sat gingerly after her workout in Tres's bedroom, while Diaz man-spread next to her.

Tres sat next to me. His large body leaned against

the door, leaving an inch of space between us. He tapped and intermittently spoke on his phone. He wasn't exactly ignoring me, but neither was he giving me his full attention.

I didn't demand it. He'd done more than enough, more than any other man would have under the circumstances. I needed to find a way to make it up to him after all this was over, assuming he still wanted me up against him.

We touched down in Vegas as the sun began to set. In a town of excesses and vices, the front of the Mohegan Casino was opulence on crack. The building was made of reflective glass with lights so bright I'm sure they could be seen from space. Crowned on the top of the building were awnings of blood red, sun yellow, and turquoise blue that brought to mind a headdress. Crowning the roof of the building were the figures of a jaguar and a deer. Fitting for the children of gods, one of whose name translated Jaguar Deer.

Most Indian casinos were built on tribal land, which freed them from the rules of US gambling laws. The Mohegan had many casinos on tribal lands, but they also shouldered their way onto the Strip. In the midst of Italy's Venetian, Caesar's Roman Palace, and Egypt's Luxor, they'd placed a gaming establishment that shone the might of the Native American spirit.

A fountain spewed colored water before the Mohegan Casino. As we walked by, I saw precious stones decorating the floor of the waters. Inside the casino hall there were more lights everywhere. Dice rolled, cards flowed, money was shoved forward, and chips were pulled back into chests.

A plasma screen showed a pyro display interspersed with Indian warriors throwing spears at buffalo and riding wild horses bare-chested while aiming bows and arrows. The message of strength and power was clear for a once-mighty people who had been forced into crippling poverty not long ago.

The purveyors of this newfound dominance were situated up high on what looked like a mountain. The shifter twins looked down amidst the squeals and groans on the floor below them. Their lips quirked up at the sighs and moans of the pale men and women playing, and more often than not losing, their games. Their shrewd gazes spotted us at the far end of the room, and their pupils flashed. In tandem, the Mohegan chairmen turned and made their way down the stairs toward us.

The word *mohegan* meant wolf. Though the wolves of North America came from many different native tribes, all shifters identified as Mohegan. The two identical men walking toward us barely contained the predatory animals beneath their human skins.

They were dressed in tan business suits instead of the black or pinstripe suits of Wall Street, and it worked for them. They wore chokers around their necks, not ties. Their eyes were dark as granite, their cheekbones as sharp as arrowheads. Though I had never met them face to face, I knew them.

They were twins, like all shifters born of the God Twins, so I couldn't tell the chairmen apart. I knew that their names were Achak and Ahusaka, meaning *spirit* and *wings* respectively.

Their dark curtain of hair billowed behind them as they stalked toward us. It was as though a fan blew their waist-long locks, allowing strands to whip slowly and coil seductively about their eyes and lips. Every woman in the casino stopped and gawked as the twins passed by. The women bit their bottom lips as the men came forward; they licked their top lips as they caught sight of the chairmen's backsides. Hell, even I squirmed as they approached.

"Tres, the man!" said one twin as they both came to stand before us.

Tres embraced one and then the other man.

"Chak," he said, greeting the one on the left, saying his name with the soft *sh* sound. "Saka," he greeted the other man.

"It's been too long," said Saka.

"Remember that party earlier this year?" said Chak. "Those models? You were a beast."

Tres scratched at the back of his head. It was the first time I'd seen him look sheepish. Was he embarrassed of his past? I knew he had one. But it was kinda nice that he'd rather keep it quiet in front of me.

"You're coming out with us tonight, yeah?" said Saka.

"No, not this time," said Tres. "I'm here on a personal matter. This is Nia."

Both men cocked their heads to the side and looked me up and down.

"This is Nia?" said Saka.

"*The* Nia?" said Chak.

Once again I squirmed in the presence and under the scrutiny of these two. I was saved from making any small talk or delving into what had been discussed about me between these three men when there was loud throat-clearing behind me. The chairmen looked beyond me. They each lowered their eyes, but there wasn't much obeisance.

"Your Highnesses," the Mohegan twins said in unison.

Skye and Skully only glared. A clear power struggle brewed on the casino floor. Luckily, they couldn't do anything physical with so many humans about. At least I didn't think they would.

"Why don't we take you on a tour," said Saka, clearly the diplomat of the two.

We all fell in line. Well, Tres, Diaz, and I fell in line. The Balam and Mohegan stayed in step with one another. Both sets of twins not so subtly jockeying for the leadership position at the head of the group.

"We don't care about this capitalist venture you two have going here," said Skully, her voice laced with menace as she sneered at the slot machines that lined the walkway.

"As you know, Your Highness," Chak sneered right back, "our people have played games of chance and skill since the dawn of time. Even our own fathers had their ritual ball game."

"That ball game was life or death," corrected Skye.

"Yes," said Chak, "as our Mayan cousins showed with their ritual sacrifice of their people."

Skye growled. Chak smiled good-naturedly.

"As you're well aware, the US government and their Act of 1851 devastated the original peoples of this continent," said Saka. "But they didn't realize they were laying the groundwork for us to take our land and resources back. The law allowed for us to build the mechanism to do that. Because they can't rule us, we can make these casinos."

"Instead of letting American Indians suffer in poverty," said Chak, "we are buying US land with the profits and turning them back to tribal. Ironic, huh?"

"Poetic," agreed Saka.

It was an admirable effort, and it was having a positive effect. Not a wide-sweeping effect, of course. Not with Native American poverty still incredibly high. But admirable, still.

The queens didn't smile admiringly.

"There's honor in giving," said Skully. "Not in accumulating."

"We've set up casinos in over ten states, and we're looking at expanding even further," said Saka. "These casinos allow tribes to be self-sufficient. The government isn't coming to reservations and building roads and infrastructure. They're not providing health care and housing. We're doing that. We're providing jobs, not just to Mohegan, but to many human tribes. It's enabling them to pass that wealth on to the next generation and pull communities out of poverty and depression while you play in your little park in the woods. And you turn your nose up at that?"

Skye and Skully turned to each other. An unvoiced thought passed between the queens. Then they turned back to face the chairmen. The look on both of their faces was loud and clear.

"We turn our nose up at your lack of honoring the old ways," said Skye.

Saka and Chak turned to look at each other. What must have been a similar unvoiced thought passed between the chairmen. They shared a sigh and then turned back to face the queens.

"All right," said Saka. "Let's get this over with. Follow me."

With a few more steps, he led us all to a hall that spit out into a regulation-sized boxing ring.

"Clear the room," Chak called to the half dozen men and women milling about.

The room cleared in sixty seconds. When the door closed behind the last human, I turned back to see both male twins taking off their jackets.

Skully cracked her neck. Beside her, Skye rolled her shoulders. The four shifters entered the ring, each taking a corner. Diaz corralled Tres and me back to ringside, where we took seats.

"It's ceremony." Diaz shrugged at my quizzical gaze.

When it dawned on me what was about to happen, I let out an annoyed groan. "But I haven't had the chance to ask them permission to dig yet."

Diaz gave me another shrug. Then he turned and winked at his woman as she gathered her hair in a ponytail. There was no bell to start the stately proceedings. Instead, there was the loud crack of flesh meeting bone as the Mohegan and Balam clashed in the center of the ring.

CHAPTER TWENTY-ONE

Skully went for a low blow, high-kicking Saka in his nether region. The wolf protected his jewels within an inch of his life.

On the other side of the ring, Chak went straight for Skye's face with his claws. She back-stepped in her heeled boots and caught his forearm. Chak went low, swiping at her leather boots with his gators.

"Did you do the fixtures in here?" Diaz asked Tres.

Tres nodded, his eyes on the aggressive display before us all.

"It's really nice," said Diaz. "I've been thinking about doing something similar at the manor. We need something sturdy with all those cubs monkeying around."

A loud crack broke up the guys' home renovation conversation when Saka's body was tossed upward and broke said fixture.

"Maybe something sturdier?" said Diaz.

The moment Saka's body hit the ground, Skully was on him. She managed to get her claws around his throat. But Saka kicked her legs out from under her. Gaining the upper hand, he loomed over her. Grabbing her by the shoulders, he body-slammed her into the mat.

"Oh," grimaced Diaz. "That's gonna piss her off."

But I didn't have time to wait and see what Skully would do. Things were picking up between Chak and Skye. She dodged and blocked a series of his advances. Both of their long manes spun and whirled as they lunged and dipped and sprang into action.

The two stepped apart, stepping over their twins who grappled on the mat. When Chak and Skye got to the opposite corner of the ring, they threw their lower bodies into the fight, with their booted heels and knees and femurs striking into hips and sides.

"You know you owe me a new pair of sheets for defiling my bed," said Tres.

It took me a moment to realize he wasn't speaking to me.

"*Pfft.*" Diaz blew out a harsh breath. "Like you haven't sullied that bed enough with a different woman every night."

Tres's eyes narrowed and his mouth gaped. He made a not-so-subtle head nod toward me.

Diaz frowned and then made the same harsh sound through his lips again. "It's not like she doesn't know your past and who she's climbing into bed with."

Tres's chin dipped as he met my gaze. He cleared his throat and fidgeted with the button of his business suit jacket. I wanted to tell him that it was fine, that Diaz was right; I knew he had a past.

I was a bit surprised at my lack of jealousy. I was pretty possessive with my things, as evidenced by the fact that I hoarded my prized possessions on a desert island. But I didn't have a chance to say anything with the fight picking up in the ring.

Skully and Saka were back on their feet. Skully landed a powerful right hook across his chiseled jaw. Blood splattered.

Saka whipped back and got an elbow in Skully's solar plexus. She doubled over, but only for a second. When she rose, there was blood trailing out of her grinning mouth.

"By the gods, she's beautiful when she bleeds," sighed Diaz.

Tres and I gave each other a look that said *And we thought we had problems.*

He wrapped an arm around my shoulder as the fight came to a close.

The four shifters sat or lay on the mat of the ring. Diaz rose and brought a first aid kit over. Skye brought a thick wad of gauze up to Saka's cheek. He winced as she pressed it into his darkening bruise. Chak poured antiseptic over Skully's bloody knuckles and then gave her the bottle so that she could do the same to him.

The Balam fussed over the Mohegan as they did the jaguars in their own care. They were siblings after all. It was something I would never understand about shifters.

Fighting was not only a way of life, a rite of passage, it was also a love language amongst their kind. They could tear into one another verbally or physically one moment, and then turn around and lick the wounds they'd just inflicted literally and figuratively. But at the end of the day, after the blows were dealt, they always came back to take care of one another.

I watched Chak as he bandaged Skye's knuckles.

She was the elder by centuries but you could hardly tell the age difference between them. Even though the Mohegan were wolves and the Balam were jaguars, they all favored each other in their human forms. Well, obviously, since they all had the same fathers.

Shifters bruised, but they healed quickly. There were no allergies between them. I was feeling fatigued from being around my own kind for two straight weeks. It wouldn't have been so bad if it was just one Immortal. But I'd constantly been in the presence of two nearly every day.

With the fight over, and the healing begun, I rose from Tres's loose embrace and got down to business. I figured this was the most opportune time since the chairmen had their guard down.

"You want to dig up a mound?" Saka asked. He turned to the queens. "And you call us sellouts?"

"Nia's looking for our dads," said Skye.

"They're not dads," said Saka. "Dad is an earned title by a man who sticks around and takes care of his responsibilities. They may be our birth fathers. They may be the reason that we're alive, but that's where their contribution ends."

"I'm not looking for them as much as I'm trying to gain access to Xibalba, the underworld," I said.

The chairmen looked at each other. Saka tried to raise an incredulous eyebrow, but it was too swollen and he wound up grimacing. They both turned back to me.

"What for?" asked Chak.

"There's a prophecy," I said. "A witch had a vision that two more of my kind will die before we get to the garden from whence we came. I think that garden is Xibalba."

"So you're trying to hasten someone's death?" said Chak.

"No," I said. "I'm trying to stop it."

"By making the prophecy happen sooner?" said Saka.

"Yeah," said Chak. "Wouldn't you want to keep other Immortals away from Xibalba if something bad was predicted to happen once you got there?"

I looked to the queens, who were considering this. Then I looked to Tres, who shrugged. Was I the only person who hadn't considered that eventuality?

But then I shook my head. "Prophecies are never set in stone. Living as long as we all have, we know that as a fact. I have the opportunity to try and make a change, and I'm going to take it. You'd do the same for anyone in your family."

The brothers looked up at the bruises and blood of their sisters. They all nodded.

"The International Antiquities Commission has been trying to excavate the Ohio Serpent Mound for years," said Saka.

"They believe we buried our dead there," said Chak. "But it was made by the Fort Ancients to honor the Hunter and Jaguar Deer."

Hunter and Jaguar Deer were other names for the God Twins.

"There are no bones or anything down there," Chak continued.

"But with it being a place of worship," I said, "the God Twins may use it to come into this world. We've noted that there are stela at the temples and mounds where there may be doors to Xibalba. They align during astronomical events. The next event is the solstice, and it's happening in just a few days."

"You think our fathers are coming to the surface in a couple of days?" asked Chak.

"I don't know about that," I said. "But we might be able to get in through the Serpent Mound's door if we can get beneath the mound and find access."

"We'll need to consult the elders," said Saka. "We're not an autocracy."

"Can you get on a conference call?" I asked.

"Some elders don't like technology." Chak eyed the Balam queens. "So it may take a few days."

"I don't have that much time," I said.

The brothers looked to each other again. Silent communication rang loud in the room. No, actually, that was a phone.

Saka rose on jelly legs and pulled a phone from his jacket pocket. His thumb went instantly to the silencer button, but he frowned down at it before depressing the button. "It's a call from Ohio."

Saka put the phone to his ear. He was too far away for me to hear the conversation, but I could tell that the other shifters heard the other end of the phone call loud and clear.

As though in choreographed unison, each of their eyebrows rose. Skye sniffed at the air, her nostrils flaring. Skully tilted her head to the side like she heard a predator off in the distance. A low growl emanated from Chak.

Saka looked each of them in the eye before his gaze came to land on me. "Someone has desecrated sacred land. You'll never guess where. It's the Serpent Mound."

My eyes widened and my head jerked back. Could it be the God Twins? Could I have the dates wrong? Did they not need an alignment to open a door? Maybe they could always come and go as they pleased. They were gods after all.

But no. The gods had been coming and going for centuries. They'd never before desecrated one of their own temples. It had to be a human.

"Did they catch the people who did it?" I asked.

"Person," said Saka, hanging up the phone. "One man. He tunneled down beneath the mound and destroyed a section below ground. The local tribe turned him over to the Mohegan. They have him in their custody. They're holding him now."

I was numb the entire flight from Nevada to Ohio. Tres kept his distance, talking with the Mohegan chairmen and the Balam queens in the office nook of his private jet. Diaz sat beside me. He held my hand in his large paw, but I didn't hear a word he said.

The moment we touched down, we immediately boarded a helicopter to get to the mound quicker. We'd chased the sun across the continent and it was now setting once again, this time over the Ohio Valley. In just a few days the disk would rest on the head of a serpent and potentially open a door that might lead to the place of my birth. To the underworld where gods resided. Some of those gods may be my parents.

We passed over the waters of the Ohio Bush Creek. Just beyond the creek was our destination. Looking down from the sky, I saw the spiraling tail, then the three coils of the Serpent Mound. The head was an oblong circle that sat on a triangle sconce. There were seven evenly spaced coils in the open field that made up the serpent's body. But now, there was a hole between the head and the first coil.

The damage was the same as the mound I'd seen back in La Sufricaya when I'd been accosted by the jaguar toms. It was obvious that the destruction was the work of the same man.

The pilot set the copter down in the open field. The attraction was now cordoned off and closed to the public after the unthinkable vandalism. Somehow the Mohegan had managed to keep the news quiet, not that it would be much interest to the human world that a pile of ancient Indian dirt had been dug up.

We made our way to the mound and were met by more of the Mohegan. These shifter twins turned first to the queens and bowed their heads in deference. I didn't miss the nod of approval they got from Skye at the correct order of the protocol. Then the Mohegan men nodded their heads to the chairmen and placed their hands over their hearts in pledge.

I wandered away as they began talking amongst themselves. My attention was on the ground. It was a small hole. Only big enough to fit one body down below. The mound itself, the tail, the coils, and the head were not disturbed.

"He damaged the eighth coil," said the Mohegan ranger who I'd gathered was in charge of the site. "That particular tunnel between the head and the second coil has caved in."

"Eighth coil?" I asked, turning back to face the group. "There is no eighth coil."

"It's below ground," said the ranger. "The ancestors told us that when the mound was made there was a man from across the waters who helped in its construction. They allowed this man to build the eighth coil below ground. We don't know why. The information wasn't recorded. You can only see any trace of it when Venus aligns. It used to look like this."

The ranger handed the chairmen a sheet of paper. They frowned and handed it to Tres. Tres sighed as he looked down at the sheet of paper. Diaz came over his shoulder and winced when his gaze met the parchment.

I couldn't make my way over because Skye and Skully beat me to it. The queens both smirked when they saw what was on the document.

When I finally was able to shoulder my way through, I had to look down to make sure I hadn't fallen through the man-sized hole in the ground, because it felt like the ground shifted under me. I'd never once in my life fainted. But I came very near to it today.

The shape on the paper was my name. There had been an eighth coil. But it could only be seen by glancing at it from a particular perspective. It was a U-shape just like the other coils, but with a divot where Venus would sit when it made its passage over the land.

"Where is he?" I asked.

They led us to a gatehouse shortly beyond the property. Inside, sitting in a chair with mud-caked boots and an earth-stained shirt, was Zane.

His arms were crossed over his chest. There was a look of nonchalant boredom on his face. On his arms were scratches from long claws that were already healing. A slice rent through one of his pant legs. But the blood had stopped. Two Mohegan in wolf form stood guard, even though Zane made no move to escape.

He looked up as we all filed into the room. Skye and Skully threw him thumbs-up signs. Diaz shook his head. Tres's face was carefully blank. The chairmen looked him over with interest.

Zane dismissed each one with a blink and an eye roll. When his gaze met mine it flickered. Not with brightness or joy. With dark wariness. And then he blinked once more, rolled his eyes, and turned away from me too.

So many questions went through my mind. But what came out of my mouth was indignation. "You destroyed a piece of history."

He didn't respond.

"That was you too, in Guatemala. The mound at La Sufricaya? Why? Why would you do that?"

But I knew why he'd done it. Zane had once said to me that he could never forget me as I had forgotten him over the centuries. He'd said that he would always remember because he put me into his art. He wasn't just a painter and a sculptor. He didn't only confine his work to the page and metal. He'd drawn me in the very earth, a monument for all of time that would shine with the movement of the celestial bodies in the heaven, never to be forgotten until the end of time.

I gulped at the realization. "So this is what, like, your break-up box?"

I'd never had one myself—a break up box where I kept tiny remembrances of a relationship gone south. I'd never had a real relationship with another man that I would want to burn, as I'd seen other women do after a bitter ending. I hadn't had the need to keep anything Zane gave me because the things he gave me were often on display around the world. I could walk into a museum and see a painting or statue with my likeness just about anywhere I wound up.

With my relationship with Zane, I'd never felt the need to have keepsakes that I kept on my person. Zane and I didn't deal in trinkets, not when we prized time together more than possessions. The only thing that I'd ever wanted from him was his attention and his touch. He gave me those in as many ways as he could even through the allergy. Other than that, the only things I tried to hold on to were the memories of us. And those constantly slipped through my fingers.

"You're destroying everything in your life that had to do with me?" I asked. "Because you were trying to forget me? Trying to forget us?"

He shook his head, eyes locked on the ground.

"You have a habit of thinking everything is about you, Nia."

I tensed, balling my hands into fists. I'd already warned Zane about his incessant, hurtful name calling. "When my name or my face is involved, I tend to do that."

Zane stood and faced me, his nostrils flaring. I squared off against him, my gaze blazing. The Mohegan wolves looked between us, then at their chairmen. They didn't wait for permission; the wolves wisely backed off and got out of our way.

"Maybe if you give me some space," Zane said through gritted teeth, "I can create something new. But you keep following me around."

"Oh, you think I'm here stalking you?"

"You always find me. Always." He began ticking off on the fingers of his right hand. "Egypt. Greece. China. Central America. North America."

I opened my mouth to launch into him. From my peripheral vision, I watched the Balam and Mohegan back up, clearing space to give us room to fight. But they were about to be disappointed.

My shoulders deflated. I just didn't have it in me any longer. I'd been fighting so hard these past couple of weeks to save this man, to hold onto even a sliver of what we once had. But I saw now that we weren't going to make up.

We were just going to keep swiping at each other and ignoring that the other was bleeding. He was going to keep tearing at the Band-Aids I was trying to put on him. He wasn't going to lick my wounds. He wasn't going to let me anywhere near him to pour antiseptic on the places where he hurt—not the mud from beneath his fingernails, or the scrapes on his shins, or that speck of dirt on his forehead.

"You push me away and then you come after me," he was saying. "And somehow I'm the one who winds up groveling for your affection. I'm done."

And just like me, his shoulders deflated. He wasn't even yelling anymore. His voice was quiet, resolved. The fight was all gone out of him.

"I'm so done," he said quietly.

And he was. I saw it in his eyes. It was the first time he'd looked at me in weeks, really looked at me.

In the reflection of his gaze, I was just a woman. It was as though the scales had fallen from his eyes. I was no longer a piece of art he wanted to capture and mold. I felt naked, exposed, and so vulnerable standing there with the reverence gone from his gaze.

The worst part was that there was nothing I

could do. Zane didn't argue when he thought he was right. He was silent. He was done with me.

He turned to the Mohegan chairmen. "What I destroyed was something that I had crafted with my hands and my spirit, meaning that it was my own to destroy. Am I free to go?"

The brothers looked to each other. Then they looked to their sisters. With no one giving a clear answer, Zane marched out the door.

I stood staring after him. The fight may have gone out of me, but the fear that something bad was about to happen to him wasn't. Panicked, I turned to Diaz.

Diaz nodded without the need for any words. But before he could take a step to the door, Tres placed a hand on his chest.

"Let me," Tres said, and stepped toward the door to trail behind Zane.

It took five seconds before my feet set in motion after both of them. Watching Tres move in the shadow behind Zane, I knew deep in my gut that this would not end well.

CHAPTER TWENTY-THREE

"Zayin, wait," Tres called out as he stepped out into the settling darkness.

It took a moment for my eyes to adjust and find Zane. His long legs ate up the ground as he put distance between himself and the rest of us.

"The last person I need to deal with is you," Zane growled over his shoulder at Tres.

"Listen," said Tres as he caught up to Zane. He reached out, but thought better and pulled his hand back. "I know you're upset, but—"

Zane whirled around. Tres had been right to retract his hand. If he hadn't, I doubt it would still be attached to his body in the face of the seething anger coming off of Zane.

And it was all my fault. I had hurt this beautiful, creative, strong man and broken his spirit.

"Upset? I was upset when you decided to go cut down a witch's Huluppu tree because you liked the way it smelled. Meanwhile, I'm the one who got torn up by her magical pet bull."

Huluppu trees? Witches? Magical bulls? What did that have to do with me?

"That was thousands of years ago," said Tres. "And it was your idea."

Thousands of years ago? Wait. Were they talking about their time in Uruk, back when Tres was King Gilgamesh and Zane was Enkidu, his partner in crime?

"Hard to forget," said Zane. "I still have the scars from the bull."

Huh. He did. There was a scar on his left butt cheek. I'd always assumed it was a birthmark. He'd never said.

"I can't believe you're still mad about that," said Tres.

"Mad?" said Zane. "I was mad when I gouged out your eye in Egypt."

Tres had often referred to Zane as Setuk, who humans believed was the Egyptian god of war. In one of the Egyptian stories of the gods, Setuk had poked out the god Horus's eye in battle.

In my head, puzzle pieces were falling into place. Bits and pieces fired rapidly in my mind. Enkidu and Gilgamesh, Setuk and Horus, Achilles and Paris, Zayin and Tresor.

"You're no innocent," Tres was saying. "You sent a horse full of Romans after me."

"After you stole away the one thing that meant the most to me in the world."

"I didn't steal her," said Tres. "She came willingly."

Oh great. Now it *was* about me. But not really.

I had to take a seat as I remembered the depth of the friendship between these two Immortal gods. The epic fights that they'd had. The unbreakable loyalty they'd shared over centuries.

"What kind of man does that to his own brother?" Zane spat out at Tres.

"There you go." Tres threw up his hands and tilted his head back to the sky as though asking for divine intervention. "You always make me out to be the bad guy when you're no prize if she keeps leaving you."

Now Zane spread his arms, taking a few steps as

he began backing away again. "Well I'm out of the running. So you can go over there and take her."

He pointed a dismissive forefinger at me, pausing to find my gaze. My throat worked as he turned that roiling anger on me. But the moment his gaze met mine, the fight went out of him once more like a rough, forceful breeze from a door slamming shut. He shook his head as though trying to brush it off. His hand fell and he turned to go.

I wrapped my arms around myself and watched him go. My eyes blurred at the sight of his back. I felt like I was going to throw up as he took another, and yet another, step away from me. But I couldn't make myself move to chase after him.

"Wait." Tres did reach out and grab Zane's arm this time.

Zane yanked away. "Take your hands off me, you *sard*-ing *putain*."

I rose from my seat then. If Zane was resorting to ancient curse words, he was about to blow his top.

"Calm down, and watch your language." Tres rounded on him and blocked his path. His tone was steel, but Zane would not bend.

"I'll say whatever the *futuo* I want and go wherever the *ayreh feek* I want."

Zane took another step, shoulder-checking Tres.

But Tres wouldn't let him pass. The two men glared at each other. The air was saturated with hundreds of years of hurt and hostility.

The immobility fell from my body and I took a step. I didn't get more than that one step. Something held me back.

"Let them go at it," said Diaz. "This has been a long time coming. It's not like they can kill each other. Believe me, they've tried in the past."

I couldn't tell who threw the first punch. The crackle of thunder rent the air. And then, for a moment or two, everything was a blur. Behind me, the Mohegan cast bets on the fight from the side of the grassy arena. When the odds weighed heavily in Tres's favor, the queens got in on the action, throwing their money behind Zane.

Out before us stood a massive Goliath versus, well, an equally massive Goliath. Zane and Tres were of the same height. Where Tres was all bulky strength, Zane was a lean bunch of muscles.

Tres made a straight line for Zane, like the mathematically exacting engineer that he was. Zane rounded Tres in a zigzag fashion like the innovative artist that he was. As he leaped into the air at Tres's side, Zane's facial muscles bunched at his eyes and around his mouth as his clenched fist landed across Tres's temple with a deafening crack.

Tres backed up a few steps at the impact. He shook off the blow just in time to block Zane's next strike. With an evasive maneuver, Tres was able to land his own punch in Zane's gut.

Zane's body caved as he heaved from the hit. His shoulders went forward but he used that momentum to shove Tres's chest. Lifting his foot, Zane aimed for Tres's kneecap. The heel of Zane's muddy boots missed the front of Tres's gleaming designer dress shoes by only a fraction. Tres advanced now with a kick to Zane's side, but Zane managed to sidestep and counter-attacked. They were moving so fast that the leaves blew off the trees above them in the calm night.

Anger and betrayal burned brightly in Zane's eyes. Guilt and shame shone through on Tres's face. The emotions were equal weights as the men thrust into each other, working out their issues with their fists instead of with words.

Zane got his hands around Tres's throat. But Tres reversed their positions and pummeled Zane into the ground. As they went blow for blow, it felt like the earth was shaking. I couldn't take it any longer. I stood, racing into the fray, and stepped up between them.

"Enough," I shouted.

But they didn't hear me. Or they weren't listening. Either way, they ignored my directive and stepped around me. I stepped between them again and caught the back of Tres's elbow on my cheek.

The impact rattled my brain, and I sank to my knee. My ears rang, not with a bell sound, but with the rasp of shocked and anticipatory gasps from the peanut gallery. At least the cracking sound of blows being thrown stopped.

Strong hands came around me, helping me to stand. "Oh, Theta, I'm sorry. Here, let me see—"

But Tres's hand never made it from my forearms to my cheek. With his hand in midair, his body was sent flying back across the grass. He landed with a loud thud.

Having dispensed of Tres, Zane turned back to me. He reached out with both hands and cradled my face with his palms. Fingertips that only a few seconds ago had delivered violence held me gently. Dark eyes, which had been hard only a second ago, were soft as they gazed into mine. Eyes that had looked at me with such disdain for days were filled with concern and tenderness.

I wanted to cry. I was crying. The wetness of a few tears pooled around Zane's thumb as he tilted my chin to examine the damage that had been done. But I'd forgotten about the pain from a moment ago, the pain from the last few days and weeks.

He was back. My Zane. Here was the man that I'd loved for longer than I could remember. With all the years we spent apart from each other, I had never missed him more intensely than I missed him now, when his body stood pressed against mine, open and vulnerable.

He looked into my eyes. Unvoiced thoughts passed between us, but I knew what he was asking. *Are you okay?* In that moment, with my face throbbing, and my feelings hurt, and my mind muddled, and my gut filled with fear of the unknown, yeah. Yeah, I was okay.

Zane's thumb tracked across the spot where Tres had struck. I winced. In the blink of an eye, his gaze shuttered. His pupils darkened. The line of his mouth hardened. The anger and rage returned, giving me whiplash.

The gentle cradle of his fingers on my face released. He turned to the side where he'd flung Tres and his hands balled into fists once more.

Tres sat up on his ass. His knees were bent, his

long arms resting on his kneecaps. As Zane let me go and turned to him, Tres hopped to his feet and held up his hands in surrender.

"Z, that was an accident."

Zane's feet set in motion, but he didn't approach Tres. He walked in the opposite direction toward the line of trees. We all turned from Tres to watch him, our heads moving left and right like we were viewing a tennis match.

Tres's brows rose in surprise at the apparent retreat, only to rise high to the sky a second later at the loud tear of a tree's roots being torn from the ground. Zane turned back to him with the trunk in his hands. Our heads all swiveled back to Tres.

"Zane," said Tres, raising a finger in his defense. "Stop playing around."

Our heads swiveled back to Zane. He did not look like he was playing at anything. He walked purposefully to Tres holding onto the roots of the massive tree. Acrimony and intention were brighter than the moonlight in his laser-focused glare.

"Zane?" I said from where I stood. I had the good sense not to run between them this time. "Zane, stop. I'm fine."

Zane did not stop.

Tres lowered his warning finger and smirked as

Zane continued to advance. "Z, man, you're not going to hit me with that tree."

Zane lifted the tree like a batter preparing to hit the ball out of the park.

"Zayin, you better not hit me with that—*oof.*"

All heads turned to where Tres flew. For the second time tonight, his body flew like a well-pitched ball that had been hit out of the park. We all turned back to Zane as he tossed the tree aside like a discarded bat.

"You crazy mother—" The rest of the statement was muffled as Tres brushed branches and mud from his suit. "You wanna see crazy? I'll show you crazy."

Tres charged, and this time they really went at it. The fighting went on for another quarter of an hour. There was nothing I could do but resume my seat next to Diaz until both men collapsed from the blows, bloodied and blue. In the end, the Mohegan decided it was Zane who won based on technical points, with the innovative use of the tree garnering him the win. That meant the men lost and the queens won, but fair was fair.

A first aid kit was produced. Diaz and the Mohegan went over to reset bones. Skully took to wiping up the blood from each man. I stood at the edge, looking from one lover to the other, unable to decide who to tend to. But it looked like they didn't need me to interfere. Because, like in Troy and probably in other times I didn't remember, this fight was not about me.

"Sorry about the bull biting your ass," Tres mumbled around a swollen lip. "I should've had your back."

Zane shook his head and then winced as a bone cracked that probably should not have. "Well, I'm not sorry about your eye back in Egypt. You deserved that."

"Yeah," agreed Tres. "Yeah, I did."

After a brief pause, Zane admitted, "The horse wasn't my idea. But I didn't stop Menelaus from sending it in either."

"I should've told you I had feelings for her." Tres's gaze found mine.

"I knew you did." Zane did not look up at me.

"It was a dick move, trying to move in on your girl. And I'm sorry."

"It sure as hell was. That's one I'm not ready to forgive you for. At least not in this century." Zane brushed Skully's helping hand away and rose on creaky knees. "Try me sometime next century. Hopefully, I'll have forgotten all about it by then."

He headed in my direction, but he still wouldn't look at me. I wanted to reach out to him. Just for another glimpse of the man I once knew. But I knew I wouldn't reach him beneath the cuts, the bruises, and the open wounds.

"These allergies are getting to me," Zane said as he passed me. "I think it's best if we all spend some time apart."

CHAPTER TWENTY-FOUR

I didn't sleep for the next two days. Every time I closed my eyes, the nightmares would assault me. Even when I blinked during the daylight hours, I saw Zane falling away from me into darkness. But that sight wasn't a dream. It had been real.

He'd walked away from me two nights ago. He'd taken a sledgehammer to what had once been between us and hacked at the foundation until it had caved in.

With Tres, he'd shouted and fought. As the dust had settled and they each took their corners, it looked like, eventually, their stupid little brotherhood would heal. But to me he gave the silent treatment and the cold shoulder. I think our bond was irreparably broken. The pieces so shattered that he no longer saw a shard of hope to make it whole, or even a semblance of what it once was, ever again.

I turned over in the bed I was allotted at the Mohegan lodge in Ohio, preparing for the work of the new day. The lodge was a few miles from the mound. Like the last two days, I spent this one excavating the Serpent Mound. The Mohegan had closed the attraction to the public. This allowed me the freedom to roam. The IAC would have had a cow if they knew I was being allowed unprecedented access to one of the sites they'd been trying to get their scientific hands on for decades.

The elders had met and refused to let me dig. They decreed that no more damage could befall the site. It might anger the God Twins.

So I used the resistivity meter to take an X-ray of the subterranean floor to see what was beneath the mound. Contrary to what the Fort Ancients had told the Mohegan, there were a few bones down there. But that was the original purpose of most mounds. They were created for religious, ceremonial, residential, and burial purposes. Whoever was buried here had to be of great importance, likely the chiefs of the native tribe or maybe even a few Mohegan themselves.

As I explored the underground world while walking above, I kept coming back to the collapsed U-shape tunnel that Zane had once created and then destroyed. Had I not seen the original scan I wouldn't have known what it was. It was completely unrecognizable. I stared for hours trying to make out the shape of me. Admittedly I was having a bit of an existential crisis.

That night, like the previous two, I spent curled up in the bed. I could hear the Mohegan going on their runs. I felt Diaz's presence but he kept his distance, knowing I needed to heal emotionally as well as physically from all the close contact with my kind.

Skye and Skully had left me alone the first two nights, but they forced their way in now to intrude on my brooding. I didn't want to have to talk with them. I knew where their loyalties lay. They were going to shove me back toward Zane. The problem was I didn't think he was going to hold still and catch me.

I remained mute for the first half hour of the twins' nagging, letting them fuss over me and fight between themselves about what to watch on the sixties-style boxed television set. They started watching reality programming of singers and their girlfriends and sidekicks, of basketball players and their wives. When they changed the channel to a family of well-endowed sisters who got tons of accolades for spending their days doing nothing at all but tapping on their cell phones, I decided enough was enough. I grabbed for the remote and turned off the television.

"Go on," I said. "Out with it."

Skye and Skully both looked at me quizzically and remained mute. Oh, they thought they were so smart. Pulling the old reverse psychology bit on me? Well, that wouldn't work.

"You think I should go after him, don't you? But I don't even know where he is or if he'll have me."

"He's back in Vegas at the Mohegan Casino," said Skye.

"And of course he'll have you," said Skully. "You saw how he took a tree to the gut for you."

"Not many men would do that."

"My Diaz would. And then I'd rip off the arms of the bastard who'd hit him."

My mouth fell open. I had to shake the disorientation from my brain. "Wait, are you talking about Tres? But you're both Team Zane."

"Oh, we are," they said in unison.

"So...I don't get it?" I said, truly confused that they weren't advocating for Zane and feeling a bit miffed at their discarded loyalty. "Are you going to tell me that when you love someone you need to let them go so that they'll come back to you?"

The side-by-side mirrors frowned at me.

"No," said Skully. "When you love someone you fight for them."

"It looks like Zane's done fighting," said Skye.

I inhaled sharply, like they'd swung a tree trunk into my gut. They waited for me to say anything more, but there were no words. They were right. Zane had stopped fighting for me. Was I ready to stop fighting for him?

The sisters turned the TV back on as I stewed over their words. I barely noticed when they rose and left the room for their nightly run. I was just about to head out myself in search of fresh air when the phone rang.

I wasn't sure which picture of a dark-haired, liquid-brown-eyed man I wanted to see. When a blonde-haired, blue-eyed woman's picture popped up on my phone, a sense of joy flooded me. My heart pounded in my chest as I pressed TALK.

"Hey, girl, hey," I said into the receiver.

Loren was exactly the girlfriend I wanted to talk to. It was a well-known fact that few would openly admit to, but women went to certain girlfriends when they wanted advice. We all knew the advice that a particular girlfriend would give before she said anything. Most times it wasn't advice we were looking for, just confirmation of the decision we'd already made.

Loren had been by my side when Zane and I had broken up earlier this year. She'd raised an eyebrow at me when I'd decided to give up men altogether. She'd been with me as I'd made bad decisions in Budapest. She'd also shoved me into Tres's arms a couple of weeks ago.

I settled back into the bed, preparing to tell her about the latest pretzel I'd gotten myself bent out of shape over. But then the sound on the other end made me pause. "Loren? What? What is it?"

I'd never heard my best friend cry. Not once during the year that I'd known her, and we'd been through some pretty trying times together. Loren had learned her true ancestry last month. She was a descendant of Sir Galahad of the Arthurian Court. She was also a witch and had recently come into her powers. Now she was in the midst of becoming an official Knight of the Round Table, but apparently,

Arthur and his merry band were being chauvinistic jerks.

"Oh, sweetie, I'm gonna go and charter a plane right now," I said. "I'll be there by tonight."

The idea sounded great. It meant I could put away my problems and focus on hers. I would gladly light into those knights and their chivalric crap that was obstructing my bestie from taking her rightful place at the Round Table, all because she had breasts. I wasn't ignoring the part about where she'd nearly gotten a witch killed by running headfirst into danger. Her crying told me that she'd learned her lesson.

"No," Loren said, getting out the last of her sniffles. "Don't do that."

I wanted to argue. I wanted to run away. But I couldn't. I had to face my problems with the men in my life, just as she had to face hers.

"You and I both have a habit of running away from our pasts," I said. "I'm there with you—in spirit. 'Cause I'm on the other side of the world and all. But you have to do this. You have to see it through. If you don't, you'll hate yourself."

If I left this all behind and ran away I'd hate myself. Zane had once told me I ran when things got tough. I couldn't blame him for not sticking around for me this time. When had I shown him that I'd fight for him?

"But," I said, bringing it back around to my best friend, "let Artie know that I will charter a plane and kick his Celtic ass if he makes you cry again."

"I can't do that," Loren said. "I can't leave my room."

There was a brief pause. "Wow, so they actually went medieval on your ass."

That got a laugh out of her. It got a laugh out of both of us.

"So what's going on with you? You still with the Broody Billionaire? Or did that Fine Frenchman find a way back into your bed?"

"I'm alone."

Now she gave me a brief pause. "Okay. Like a women's empowerment thing? Or you're just making them both stew?"

"No stewing. I think I should be by myself right now at this point in my life."

"We're back to that. Sweetie, I know you are woman and hear you roar, but after you get out of the jungle or the desert or wherever you've adventured off to, you're the type of woman who wants to have a man to go home to."

"And you think that man should be Tres?"

I could hear her shrug on the line. "You know my stance on monogamy. It's a cute idea and all. Honestly, I think Tres is a great distraction, but at the end of time, I always imagined you'd be back with Zane. You two have been together for thousands of years, after all."

The world was not making sense anymore. The queens were pushing me to Tres. My best friend was pushing me back to Zane. I got off the phone with Loren and crawled off the bed.

I looked out the window at the moon. I heard the howls of the shifters in the night. I could see the head of the Serpent Mound off in the distance.

I'd spent much of my life digging up the past. I never had much concern for the future. But now it was all I could think about.

Loren was right. I loved to go off on my adventures. I didn't like being alone when I got back home, even on my island. I wanted to share my findings with someone. The truth was, I had a lot of someones.

I had my best friend to go on adventures with. I could swing by Greece and go shopping with Demeter. I could come down to the jungle and go on hunts with the queens.

Those were the relationships I needed to focus

on when I came back from my adventures. No one would get hurt if I put more time and attention into those relationships. I just needed to go on one more adventure to make sure that no one else I loved got hurt.

And tomorrow, when the sun set, I'd make sure of that. I was completely exhausted after having come to this new decision. I lay my head on the pillow and slipped into a dreamless sleep.

It was time. The sun was making its way lower and lower toward the horizon and the crown of the serpent's head. I knew this was happening, but I couldn't see it for myself.

We weren't on the mound, we were at the Ohio Bush Creek. The elders had granted me access, but not through the top of the mound. Luckily, I'd found another way in.

"What if they're down there?" said Skye. She pressed her palms together in a prayer pose beneath her chin.

"They were in the north recently." Skully scratched at her heart until her claw snagged in the fabric of her shirt. "Saka said they found a pair of ten-year-old wolves a couple of months ago. They'll probably hit Canada next."

"Yeah," said Skye. "If nothing else, those deadbeats are consistent in being wholly unpredictable and not sticking around for long."

The queens leaned against each other as they watched the sun inch closer and closer to the horizon. Still feigning nonchalance, they fussed over their clothing and their hair as though they were meeting an important figure for the first time. I felt a tingling in my limbs as the time approached to go down into the creek and surface beneath the mound. Before the night was over, I might not only have the answers I was after, I might also come face to face with my own father, or mother.

I felt the tickle at the back of my neck announcing the nearness of one of my kind. Three days apart from Tres and Zane had restored me to my former strength. Still, my heart beat rapidly and I felt a bit lightheaded at their approach. I wasn't sure who I wanted to see when I turned around.

I chickened out and didn't turn. I didn't need to. Strong arms came around me and held me tightly.

"*Hola, manita.*"

I leaned back into Diaz's warm embrace. He'd kept his distance for the past three days as well. But he was going down into the mound. Not only because I was going but also because Skully and Skye had decided to come too.

I didn't ask if he'd heard any word from either Tres or Zane. I couldn't focus on my love life right now. It was all about the business at hand.

First I had to get beneath the Serpent Mound. Next, I had to find an entryway into Xibalba. If I made it there, I'd later have to find my way back. And then, finally, I'd deal with my relationship problems.

Some might look at that as stalling. But I really couldn't give a care. That is, until I heard the crunch of tires on gravel.

A sleek stretch limo pulled up. The panels were blacked out, but I knew who was in the car before the doors opened. A pair of snake-skin cowboy boots hit the pavement, followed by a pair of steel-toed leather boots. The Mohegan chairmen looked even more delectable in jeans than they did in business suits.

The men made their way to us, but my gaze stayed focused on the open car door. Tres stepped out of the car last. He, too, was in jeans and a dark shirt that complemented his toasty skin.

"You were gonna leave without us, *hermanitas*?" said Saka with a fake pout on his handsome face.

"Didn't think you cared about meeting our fathers," said Skye.

"We don't," said Chak. "But if there's an opportunity to tell those bastards off, we want in."

"We're the eldest," said Skully. "If they're down there, we're telling them off first."

As the siblings bickered over who would lay into their fathers first, Tres came up to me.

"You came," I said.

"I wanted to make sure you were okay." His gaze tracked over me, but he kept his hands to himself. "And that you didn't do anything stupid down there."

I grinned, and he mirrored the look. Still, neither of us reached out for the other. Tres's gaze slid away from mine as he tried to look around out of the corner of his eye.

"He's not here," I said. "He hasn't been back since that night."

Tres's gaze came back to mine, and the corners of his eyes widened slightly. "I'm actually surprised."

"Because you thought we'd be back together by now?"

Tres smiled sadly and gave a small shrug of his

right shoulder. He reached out and tilted my chin up, looking for the damage that had been done to my cheekbone. It had healed before that night was over. Satisfied, he let me go and returned his hand to his pocket before answering me.

"Together intimately?" He shrugged his left shoulder. "Together as in made up? Yes. In my experience, you two don't stay apart for too long."

"If you truly believe that, then why even bother pursuing me?"

He shrugged both his shoulders this time and gave a head waggle.

"It doesn't matter," I said. "I don't think it'll be that simple this time with me and Zane. Probably not ever again. He's really hurt."

Tres studied me quietly for a moment. "One thing I know about our kind, even though we have an adverse reaction to each other, we can't seem to stay away. He forgave me. Partially. He'll forgive you, entirely. One day. It's just in his nature."

"I thought you said he had a jealous nature."

"You did see him hit me with a tree, right?"

"I did. It's kinda funny now, looking back on it."

"I'm glad you're entertained by my pain."

He was grinning, but my smile slipped. "I don't want to hurt you."

Tres winced. "Why do I feel like we're about to have *the talk*?"

"You said the past will always be between us," I said.

"Are you breaking up with me, Theta?"

"Right now, I'm trying to put the pieces of myself back together. And when I'm done with that task, I need you to know that there will be space in my heart for both of you."

He raised an eyebrow.

"Get your mind out of the gutter, Mohandis. Not like that." I swatted at him playfully. "I mean, I forgot that we were family. I forgot that we all used to be friends. I want to spend some time remembering that, and reconciling the good and the bad of all three of us."

Shadows darkened the space between Tres's eyes and cheeks. I knew it wasn't a change in his mood. The sun had sunk lower. I swallowed as I looked toward where I knew the disk would set on the serpent's head. My heart beat a little faster not knowing where Zane was.

"You still think he's in danger?" Tres asked.

I closed my eyes. Even with that brief second, the darkness I saw scared me. I opened my eyes and nodded.

"Well," said Tres. "Let's go into the belly of a snake to save his sorry ass."

We headed away from the road and toward the creek. With my resistivity meter, I'd discovered that there was a tunnel that led from the waters to the mound. That made sense as there was no access point on the grassy knoll of the serpent's body itself.

Tres, Diaz, and I waited until the shifters changed their form. Once the Balam and Mohegan were in furs, we all waded into the water. The three of us on human legs strapped a couple of oxygen tanks to our backs, just in case. We all were fast swimmers and could hold our breath a few moments longer than humans. But we weren't sure what we'd find as we got deep underground.

On the surface, the waters were still. That saying about still waters running deep was all too true. With the help of my archeological tools, I'd learned that in some spots the creek was forty-five feet deep. I'd also seen that at a certain spot there was a passageway that led directly to the Serpent Mound.

I strapped on my headlamp and handed one to Tres and Diaz as well. The shifters, like other nocturnal animals, could see in the dark, but not in the blackness of deep waters. As the light from above receded, the lamps were all we had to rely on.

We swam down deeper and deeper, shoving water out of our way to descend. Sea creatures scattered out of the light. The jaguars and wolves scurried ahead of us, their bodies going faster than our human forms.

Soon we entered a narrow passageway. As we squeezed into the tunnel, chunks of the ceiling began to fall around me. It was like brown snowfall. The debris was like a swirling of a tornado. It fogged the light and I couldn't tell which way to go.

Before panic could set in, I felt arms tugging on me. I stopped struggling against the current and let Diaz pull me to safety. By the time I was free of the dirt storm I was covered in sediment. Once through the underground avalanche, I did a couple of barrel rolls to get the sediment off of me.

We took off again when I was clean of dirt and only the waters clung to me. We all made it through and emerged in an underground pocket of air. I removed the mask and took a deep breath. When my eyes adjusted I realized I could see as clearly as if it were a bright, moonlit night.

The interior of the cave was illuminated. But I couldn't determine the source of light. It was blue and shimmery. Whatever it was I knew it couldn't be manmade.

I was shaking. Not because I was cold. My body temperature didn't fluctuate like a human's. I was shaking because it was all becoming too real. I was close. I could feel it in my bones.

"Is that what you're looking for?" asked one of the Mohegan. I knew it was Saka by the marking of the wings on his back.

It took me a moment to follow the trajectory of where his finger pointed. Instead my gaze stayed locked on the shifter, and I shuddered for a completely different reason. He'd shifted back into his human form, and what an *au naturel* form it was.

Tres cleared his throat beside me.

I shook myself and concentrated on Saka's finger. The lights of the underground cave illuminated a rock structure. The jagged rocks hung from the ceiling. They also jutted up from the ground. A few yards away, there was a wide gash that looked as though someone could fall into the abyss.

I instinctively took a step away from the cliff and landed against Tres's wet front. His hands came to my shoulders and steadied me. I turned my gaze from the ground to the walls of the cave.

On the walls were hieroglyphs. Though I stared and stared, none of the shapes rearranged themselves in my head the way that all characters and symbols did. Even more surprisingly, I was having trouble making sense of them and determining their meaning.

But I knew I'd seen these before. It's just that the memory was buried deep. Deeper than anything in my past. Deeper than everything I thought I knew.

I spoke every language known to mankind. These were not written by man.

My attention was diverted from the wall. All of our heads turned to the voices coming from the other side of the cave. We weren't alone.

CHAPTER TWENTY-SIX

The God Twins looked larger than life, larger at least than I remembered them during my encounter with them. They were both easily eight feet tall. They were also bright. Looking at them, I felt the instinct to shade my eyes. It was like the sun was trying to break free of their skin. Despite that, I noted that their inner brilliance didn't hurt my eyes.

It took a few blinks to adjust to the glow and then I saw their features. They were more golden than bronzed. In contrast, their eyes were the pitch of night. The spots on their skin were like decorative artwork that made me itch to reach out and touch it.

They stood in front of what must have been the caved-in bit of earth from Zane's destruction. Off to the right was a doorway. There were stela on the frame that looked like the symbol for medicine: two snakes with a disk between them. It was the symbol of Venus. The door was open a crack and an even brighter light slipped through it.

"I'm telling you, Hun, those children lose respect with each generation," said one of the gods. I supposed he was Xbalanque since he'd addressed the other male as Hun, which I assumed was short for Hunahpu.

"You're right, Bal." Hunahpu nodded. "The manners are just leaching out of them."

Out of the seven of us, someone's feet shuffled and rocks kicked down the pathway. Hunahpu turned then. His gaze skated past me and landed on the four naked forms behind me.

"Did you lot make this mess?" he demanded, pointing at the sunken pile of earth.

I cringed. Though I had no memories of being raised by parents of my own, I knew that tone. When a parent put bass in their voice, it meant trouble. Problem was, these children were full-grown adults with tempers of their own. I stepped to the side to prepare for the mother of all tantrums to be unleashed in the underworld.

But as I looked behind me at the two sets of

shifter twins, I saw Skully reach for Diaz's hand and hide behind his shoulder. Skye bit her lower lip and tried to cover herself with her hands. The Mohegan were no better. Chak fidgeted and kicked stones with his big toe. Saka fussed with his hair. I think he may have put a couple of strands into his mouth and begun to chew.

"We know your mothers raised you better than this," said Xbalanque when their children remained mute. And then the god's gaze found me and Tres. "And you brought guests over without permission? It's not the time for you little Ishim to go home yet. Your parents aren't ready for you."

Ishim? My brain raced across all the documents I'd ever read to place that word, and it landed back on those that were on my desk back home on my island. The pages of the Dead Sea Scrolls I'd sequestered away spoke of the Ishim as one of the classes of angels.

Ishim, or Eshim, were said to be the class of angels closest to humans and the affairs on Earth. It was said that they were souls wrapped in fire and snow.

Aleph had always believed we were the children of angels. I'd never bought into that idea. But turning to the beings filled with glowing light, and looking past them to the doorway of light, not to mention the fact that one of those beings had just called me one of the ranks of angels, I was quickly making space for the idea in my head.

"You four will clean up this mess before you return to the surface," said Hunahpu.

"Though I'm not sure if we can even salvage this doorway." Xbalanque frowned.

The two gods shook their heads at their children and then turned away and headed in the direction of the tail of the Serpent Mound.

"Wait a minute."

Both Skye and I spoke at the same time. The gods turned back and gave their attention to their offspring.

"Is that it?" Skye said. "Is that all you have to say to us?"

The gods looked to each other. Hunahpu pursed his lips in thought. Xbalanque's brows drew together in consideration. The two brothers then faced each other. First Xbalanque, then Hunahpu shrugged. They turned back to their children and shrugged again.

"You left hundreds of children behind with no explanation, no guidance, nothing," said Skully.

"You're the children of gods," said Xbalanque.

"What rearing do you need? You should have conquered the planet by now."

"Quite frankly," said Hunahpu, "I'm a little disappointed that we aren't worshiped across the land."

"We honor your name," said Chak. "Your image crowns the palace we've created where the humans come and pay tribute."

"You can come and see it," said Saka. Then he shrugged sheepishly. "You know, if you want, and if you have time."

Skye gasped and wrinkled her nose. But then she stepped in front of her brothers, no longer concerned with her nudity. "We have lands to run wild on. They're filled with game for hunting."

"We have girls," said Saka. "Human women who will gladly attend to your needs during your stay."

"Yeah," said Skully, "but are any of your Vegas working girls virgins?"

The Mohegan and Balam tugged at the attention of the two gods who had abandoned them and their siblings at birth. I had no dog in that fight. Turning back to the open door, I reached out my hand.

"Ah-ah, little Ishim," said one of the God Twins, I wasn't sure which one.

I snatched my hand back as though I'd been about to steal a cookie from the cookie jar.

"I wouldn't do that if I were you." It was Xbalanque who spoke.

"Please," I said. "I need to go in there. To the garden."

The ancient god nodded at me. I might have been mistaken, but I thought I saw empathy in his dark eyes. I realized I was wrong. It was just a reflection of the light from the door.

"If you want to open that door"—Xbalanque looked from me to Tres to Diaz—"two of you will need to die first. There's no way around it. Those are the rules set by your parents."

CHAPTER TWENTY-SEVEN

The water from the river lapped at the rocks inside the cave. I stood staring at the door. The Mohegan and Balam were nearly out of sight as they trailed after their dads on their way to the surface. I remained behind, unable to move, so close to my goal. So close to...home.

Because I knew that's what was behind that door. I knew it with every bone in my body, with every fiber in my bones. I belonged on the other side of that door with light shining through it.

Everything I'd ever wanted to know was just on the other side of that doorway. The answer to any question I'd ever had. But I wouldn't be able to cross the threshold unless me and Tres, or me and Diaz, or Tres and Diaz died.

No. Not Diaz. He'd followed Skully out. Only Tres and I were left.

See, but here's the thing. I knew from experience that prophecies were never exactly verbatim. There had to be a way around, and I was going to find it.

I reached my hand out. Even before I moved, when I'd only had the conscious thought that I was about to make a move, the light from within stretched out to greet me. It called to me, like a siren.

I took a step, but I didn't move any further forward. I couldn't. I was tethered to someone else.

"Nia, no." Tres pulled me back, locking his arms around me.

It had been a hard tug because I didn't want to come back to him. I wanted to go forward. I had to go forward.

"You don't have to do this," he said. "We'll find Zane and we'll lock him away so that you know he's safe."

But this wasn't about Zane any longer. This was about me. I'd been on a lifelong quest for answers. Time after time, I'd dug deep, and now I realized why I always had. I'd been digging to get down here, down beneath the surface, to where I belonged.

I turned in Tres's embrace and looked into his eyes to try and make him understand. But it was as though I was looking at him with new eyes. I saw the man I'd run away with in Greece. I saw Horus from Egypt. I saw Gilgamesh from Uruk.

There were so many stories about this man. Some true. Most fabricated. I'd lived to see a lot of them. I'd read some of the fabrications. Heck, I'd written some. But I knew the truth of him.

He loved progress. He loved to surround himself with creature comforts. He felt deeply for the ones he cared about. It had torn him up inside when he decided to act on his feelings for me. He knew he would betray his best friend, but he would not betray himself. He was always truthful with himself and went after what he wanted.

I'd always admired that about him: his strength and his determination. I wrapped my arms around him now and held him tightly. After he realized I wouldn't go forward, that I was holding still, he returned the embrace.

The smell of frankincense rested on my tongue. It clung to him as always, even after going through the water. We held onto each other for long moments, until I felt him stiffen and pull away from me.

"You're about to go through that doorway," he accused. "Aren't you?"

I pulled back from him, not quite meeting his gaze. Instead, I turned back to the doorway. It had closed even more. Only a tiny sliver of light shone through, enough to just fit a body through sideways. The celestial transit that had allowed it to open from the inside out must have been nearing its end.

"Nia." Tres sighed.

"Listen, we both know that prophecies and stories and warnings aren't always what they seem. I mean, those two are called the Trickster Twins, for goodness' sake. They created this whole elaborate system of doorways. Or maybe it was created to keep them in check. They play games. This is probably another one of their tricks."

Tres did not look convinced. He shook his head. When he opened his mouth I knew that nothing good would come out of it.

"I have to try," I implored.

I took a test step away from him. When he didn't reach after me, I took another. A frustrated growl tore through him, but he still didn't stop me.

I turned back to the closing door. Reaching out my hand, I ran one fingertip over the stela that had unlocked the doorway. The moment my skin touched the frame, the ground shook.

Rocks began crumbling around me, just like they

had when we were underwater. I looked to the pile of dirt that had once been in the shape of my name. It was very likely that Zane's destruction had compromised the integrity of the structure.

We were supernatural beings, but getting buried in an underground cave that was surrounded by a body of water would be harrowing, and there was no guarantee we'd survive it.

I backed away, but when I did the ground wasn't beneath my feet. I turned to see that another crack had opened in the earth. I looked around for Tres, but he wasn't there. I looked down and saw his fingertips clutching at the ridge of earth.

I froze, like when a muscle spasm grips you in your sleep. Your body and mind are awake, but you can't move your limbs. I felt trapped inside my nightmare as Tres was slipping away from me.

He was going to die and it would be all my fault. On the bright side, I was right about the prophecy not being verbatim. On the dark side, and that would be the darkness that my immobile body peered down into, Tres was the one about to slip away from me and into the black nothingness.

I had to move. I had to do something. I had to save him.

Before I could force movement into my limbs,

something flashed at the corner of my eye. Another figure raced in front of me.

Zane dove forward and reached down. For a moment, I was afraid they both were going to go over into the darkness. It would be just my luck, as those were the words of the prophecy: two more were going to die before we were allowed inside.

But neither man went over. Zane took hold of Tres's forearm, and with a mighty heave, he pulled the other man up.

Both men fell on their backs once they were back on solid ground. The earth stopped shaking. The air was filled with their gasps and heavy breaths. I remained standing over the two, looking down as feeling returned to my limbs.

"You could've let me go," said Tres, lying on his back, looking up at the ceiling of the cave.

"Thought about it," said Zane as he came to sit up. "But if you're going to die, I want the credit. I'll be the one to push your ass over the side myself."

Tres laughed as he came to a sitting position as well. "Deal."

Tres stuck out his hand, palm facing Zane like an offering. Zane looked at it with disdain and reared back.

"We're still not good," said Zane.

But Tres ignored him. He reached over with open arms and embraced Zane. Zane didn't push him away. He rolled his eyes and his gaze landed on me.

"You came," I said.

"I knew you would try to go in."

"So, you came to stop me?"

"No," he said. "I came to save you from yourself, like always."

"Can I have a hug too?"

"No, Nova." Zane sighed. "We are not cool eith—*oof.*"

Like Tres, I ignored Zane and launched myself into his arms.

CHAPTER TWENTY-EIGHT

Tres was right. Zane could never hold on to anger for very long. It would grow inside him, and he'd tamp it down, shove it to the side, or shrug it off. Then, inevitably, something would set him off, and all the stored kindling inside him that he'd tried to ignore would go up in a blaze. But soon after the blaze went out he would be himself again, like a phoenix reborn.

The fight a couple nights ago had to have been that blaze. His anger couldn't last much longer, if there was any left at all. That thought comforted me more than the fleeting pressure of his hand on my back. We were going to be okay. We were all going to be okay.

I'd been holding on to him longer than was

acceptable for two people who had just broken up and were in the presence of the third man in the equation. But I wasn't ready to let go yet. He'd kept his distance from me for nearly two months, and in that time I'd dreamed again and again that he'd slip through my fingers and die. So, forgive me, but I held on for another moment.

Zane's hand on the small of my back felt so familiar...but in a way that transcended this moment in time. It transcended the moments he'd held me to him for the last five hundred years. The sensation lightly brushed over the times I could remember from the last two millennia. It went beyond.

The impression was so light that I couldn't touch it. Because it was light. Actual light.

Something radiated between Zane and me. I couldn't see it with my eyes, but I knew it was there. It felt like that same glow that had emanated from the God Twins after they'd come out of the door. It was coming from us. From within us.

I pulled away and looked down between us, wondering if I could see it. "Do you see it?"

"See what?" Zane asked.

But it wasn't there. My gaze turned to the side. The door was nearly closed. I might be able to get my hand in if I moved quickly.

I brought my feet under me and stood. But when I took a step forward, I got nowhere.

"Nova," said Zane, his tone a warning. "It's time to go."

I saw the light from inside shift again, dimming even more. The doorway was closing. So too was my chance to get all the answers I wanted.

"Did you hear the gods," I said. "They called us Ishim, angels."

"The Trickster Twins?" said Zane. "The ones who play pranks on mortals, steal virgins, and leave their children without a care?"

I turned from Zane to try and reason with Tres. "We're standing in front of the door. We don't know when another will open, or where. This is the closest we'll get."

"There has to be another way," said Tres.

"So what? We just wait for two more of us to die?"

Tres's eyes darkened. I knew that look. It was his calculating gaze. He turned to Zane. Zane's eyes darkened to the exact same shade. I knew their solution was not going to be in my favor.

"All right," I said. "You two get out of here. This is my decision. If anyone is going to get hurt, it'll be me."

"I knew this would happen," Zane said to Tres.

"Looks like she wants to do it the hard way," Tres said to Zane.

Both men left me out of the conversation as if I weren't standing before them. Then, finally, they turned to me in unison. Both of their handsome faces were hard and set. Their strides were long and purposeful. Four hands reached for me.

"What are you guys doing? Hey, put me down."

I'd never been manhandled before. Human men didn't really count, as I could take on a half dozen without breaking any real sweat. But two men as strong as me? This had never happened before.

They carted me away from the doorway as it shifted again. I could barely see the light from within anymore. Time was up. But I wasn't giving up.

Zane and Tres had me by my upper arms, one man on each side. I'd been pumping my feet to slow their progress away from the door. Now I stopped trying to stall them and shot out my foot. My booted heel caught Tres in the back of his knee.

"Dammit, Nia," growled Tres.

He went down, letting my arm go, which loosened Zane's grip just enough. I slipped Zane's grasp and took off.

"Nova," Zane called after me.

"Sorry," I tossed over my shoulder.

I raced back to the closing door. The hinge had nearly slipped back into place. I would barely be able to get a fingertip inside. When I reached out, something tugged my hand back. I rounded on Zane.

"I have to do this."

"That's where we disagree," he said. "No one voted to appoint you the savior of our race."

"What if it's you? What if you're one of the two who has to die before we can get the answers we need. I'm not willing to take that risk."

Zane sighed as he regarded me. "Nothing is going to happen to me."

Of course, the ground chose that moment to shake. I looked to the side to see the caved-in part of the mound, the part that Zane had destroyed, slipping into the chasm. The weight of the displaced dirt must've been too much, and the foundation gave way.

The quaking knocked me back, and my hand pressed on the stela of the two snakes holding up Venus.

The ground had shaken when the dirt of the mound fell. It tore and separated when my hand touched the stela. Zane covered me, pressing my body into the wall of the cave as the earth reshaped itself.

When I opened my eyes again we'd sunk down at least twelve feet, maybe more. Dirt coated my eyelids, obstructing my view. But one thing came into clear focus. Zane and I were on a ledge. Below was a tear in the earth. Inside the tear was a dark so absolute it made me see nightmares while I was awake.

This was my nightmare. Me and Zane on a ledge. Out in front of us was a cliff that would swallow him whole, taking him from me forever.

And it was all my fault.

I'd led him here. He'd followed me, trying to protect me. In doing so, he was going to fall to his death.

I reached out and grabbed him to me. I wrapped my arms around his torso and hung on for dear life, his life. I would not let go. Not ever.

"It's okay, *mon coeur*. We're going to be fine."

Looking to the side, I saw that the doorway was closed. The seal firmly in place. It had all been for naught.

"Nia, Zane," called Tres from above. "Here, grab my hand."

Tres leaned his long body over the side of the

ledge. Zane tried to disentangle me from him, but I wasn't having it.

"I'm going to boost you up," Zane said.

"No." I shook my head vehemently, still clutching his forearms. I knew that as long as I held onto him, he couldn't fall into the crack. "You go first."

"That's not going to happen," he said.

Zane reached around my waist and boosted me up. I wanted to struggle, but I was afraid that if I did he would fall. So I closed my eyes and held my breath, hoping that I would wake up from this horror.

"I can't reach," said Tres.

"Is there something you can drop down?" asked Zane.

I opened my eyes to the sleeve of Tres's shirt waving like a white flag of surrender. He'd taken the garment off to give us more leverage.

"Nova," said Zane. "Grab the sleeve."

But my fingers clenched around Zane's wrists. I couldn't get them to open. "I've been having these nightmares," I began.

"I know," Zane said. "Diaz told me. I'll be right behind you. I promise."

I turned and looked over my shoulder at the closed door.

"We're not going that way," said Zane. "That way is closed to us. We'll find another way. I promise."

I took a deep breath. One by one, I unfurled my fingers. I reached up and caught the cuff of Tres's shirt. Tres began to tug. The moment he did, the earth began to shake again.

Zane's hold on my waist broke. I was left dangling by the cuff of Tres's shirt. Zane was slammed back to the wall, just shy of the doorway.

"Zane." I reached out with one hand. "Here, grab my hand."

He walked over to me. Rocks fell all around us like a rain shower. The earth continued to grumble, as though in warning.

"It'll be too much weight," Zane said, nodding his head to the shirt. "I'll find another way."

"There is no other way," I insisted, my voice rising a couple of octaves, just shy of hysterical.

"Zayin," shouted Tres. "Don't pull this martyr crap right now. Grab her hand."

But Zane was right. The shirt was starting to tear as it met a jagged rock. Zane reached up to my fingertips. His gaze was wide open to me, and once more, I saw the man that I had loved for longer than I was able to count.

He smiled at me as he tilted his head left and

right, like he always did before he sat down to paint a masterpiece. But there was no paintbrush down here. No pencil. No parchment.

He was sketching me in his mind, like a memory he would have to hold onto for the rest of his life. I tried to curl my fingers around his, but he stepped back. He was out of my reach. It was exactly like he'd done in the nightmare.

"Pull her up," Zane said.

"You promised," I accused.

Zane didn't say anything. He stared mutely at me, not open to any arguments.

I looked up to Tres. Even in the dim light of the cave, I saw the shock and horror on his face. He was not focused on me. His gaze was locked with Zane's as some sort of silent communication passed between these two rival-allies, these two enemy-buddies, these two soul brothers.

In the end, Tres gave the shirt a mighty tug. I was being pulled away from Zane, up to safety.

"Give me your hand, Nia," said Tres.

But I turned back to Zane. This was not happening. This was not going to be the end. This would not be the last time I would see his face. Or hear his voice. Or see him looking at me like that.

No. The word resounded in my head. Then it was a shout in the dark.

"No."

I yanked my hand away from Tres. I let go of the shirt. I pushed away from the cliff.

And then I was falling into the darkness.

CHAPTER TWENTY-NINE

The darkness was humid and thick. It wrapped around my body like stubby, cloying fingers that slid over my skin. It gripped at my legs and flung me feet over head. I knew at any moment I could crash. Or maybe I'd simply fall forever.

But I didn't.

Strong arms snatched me from the heavy air. The arms brought me into the familiar valley of an unyielding chest. I knew this place. It was as familiar to me as the palm of my hand. It gave the same comfort and molded to my cheek just as my palm did when I was deep in thought, or reading a good book, or nodding off to sleep.

Zane clutched me to him, holding me still. He

pressed my face into his chest and cradled the back of my head, protecting me from the world falling around us. Though he shielded me, the rocks raining down around us still hurt. But not as much as his stupid grand gesture.

When the dirt shower slowed from a downpour to a drizzle, I wriggled out of Zane's hold and punched him in the chest, right in the heart.

"Ouch," he moaned.

His body caved in as he rubbed at the spot he'd cradled me in a moment ago. But I didn't care about his pain. I was livid.

"How could you do that?" I said. "How could you do that to me."

"I was trying to save your life."

"I was trying to save yours."

"Zayin? Theta?" Tres's voice boomed in the darkness above. "I hear you arguing so I have to assume you're both still alive."

"For now," said Zane. "She's trying to yank my heart from my chest."

"Yeah, like I said," said Tres. "You're both fine."

Zane leaned back against the cave wall, careful not to touch the stela on the closed door. He stared at me with wide-open eyes as he shook his head. A small smile played at his lips.

Part of me wanted to punch him again. The other part wanted to kiss him. I aimed for the middle and wrapped my arms around him again. He didn't hesitate to return the embrace.

"You knew that was my worst nightmare." I dug my nails into his shoulder blades. I hid my face in his chest, finding that spot that fit my head perfectly.

"I'm fine," he said. "We're both fine."

"Don't ever do that to me again."

"I won't. I promise." He lifted my chin so that I could see his eyes. "Truly, this time."

We stood breast to chest. Soil and sediment were the only thing in the air between us. We were so close. If it were a year ago I would be able to kiss him. But there was still so much crud between us.

Zane brushed his thumb over my cheekbone. "You would've died for me."

The thought of a life without him was unbearable. Instead of thinking of it, I closed my eyes and rested my head back in my spot.

I didn't want either of us to die. I wanted us both to live and take part in each other's lives. I didn't want to fight anymore. I wanted to be allowed back in this space whenever I wanted.

Zane pressed his lips to my forehead. He took a

deep breath that ruffled the hairs on my temple. "Okay, now let's figure out a way out of here."

We both turned to the ledge we needed to summit in order to get back to safety. The top was now even further away. Tres's shirt was the only thing visible in the dark as it hung from a jagged bit of earth on the face of the chasm.

"We're gonna have to climb," said Zane.

"We'll do it together," I said.

He nodded, lacing his fingers with mine. It was clear that we'd have to take a running leap and hope for purchase. There was no other way.

I felt him take a deep breath. I did as well. The moment we stepped away from the wall, the ground shook again.

Zane immediately brought me back into his arms. I didn't fight this time. I held onto him for dear life. Both his and mine. But our embrace did nothing to stop the seismic shock or its mortal results.

The world went topsy-turvy, turning us over and thrashing us about as we plummeted into the dark chasm. Through it all, Zane never let me go, and I held tightly to him.

In the distance, I could hear Tres calling out to us. But his voice fell further and further away as we plunged into the dark pit of death. I'd been afraid in my nightmares. I wasn't now. Because I knew Zane was with me, wrapped around me as we dropped into nothingness.

I knew that we weren't just falling. We were dying. There was nothing either of us could do to stop it. I hadn't stopped the prophecy from coming true. I'd been the harbinger of death. I'd brought it right to myself and the person I was trying to save.

The thing about dying? It hurt. At each turn, my body was impacted by sharp points, blunt edges. The worst part? I knew Zane was getting the worst of it because he'd wrapped his body around mine to shield me.

My head throbbed. It felt like my brain was blowing up like a balloon, ready to explode. But it didn't burst. Instead, I was pushed to the edges of my consciousness.

Finally, after minutes, days, years, I have no idea, my body impacted the bottom, and I knew that I was dead because I couldn't move.

It felt as though every bone in my body had broken. I'd heard the snap that severed my spine a long time ago. It had hurt the worst, and then I'd felt nothing.

I wasn't sure if my eyes were open or closed. But I felt the light all around me. It was the same light that had shone through the doorway. I knew it instinctively. Those damn tricky twins. They'd said we'd have to die in order to get to the other side. They'd said nothing about going through the actual door.

It took me a while, but I was finally able to actually open my eyes. When I did, I remembered. I remembered everything.

The adventure concludes in
Eden's Garden
Book Five of the Nia Rivers Adventures.

Grab your copy of the final, climactic, life-altering adventure today!

Have you started the Misadventures of Loren yet?
Now's the perfect time to read Book One,
The Spear of Destiny
as Loren starts her quest to become Dame Galahad.

Lover of fairytales, folklore, and mythology, Ines Johnson spends her days reimagining the stories of old in a modern world. She writes books where damsels cause the distress, princesses wield swords, and moms save the world.

You can sign up for her mailing list and receive alerts and free reads at http://bit.ly/InesReaders.

The Nia Rivers Adventures

Dragon Bones

Demeter's Tablet

Templar Scrolls

Serpent Mound

Eden's Garden

The Misadventures of Loren

Spear of Destiny

Ring of Gyges

Hammer of God